African Studies
Educational Resource Center
100 International Building
Michigan State University
East Lansing, MI 48824

 **To Tangle
With Tarzan**

To Tangle With Tarzan

Seven Short Stories and an Epic

Chudi Uwazurike

Africa World Press, Inc.
P.O. Box 1892
Trenton, New Jersey 08607

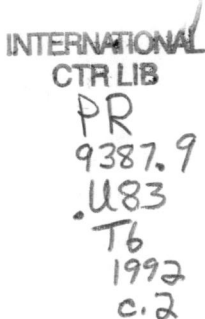

 Africa World Press, Inc.
P.O. Box 1892
Trenton, NJ 08607

© Chudi Uwazurike, 1992

All rights reserved. No part of this publication may be reproduced, stored in a retrieval system or transmitted in any form or by any means electronic, mechanical, photocopying, recording or otherwise without the prior written permission of the publisher.

Cover design by Goddy WichenDu C.
Book design by Jonathan Gullery
This book is composed in Hiroshige

Library of Congress Catalog Card Number: 91-71025

ISBN: 0-86543-247-3 Paper
       0-86543- 246-5 Cloth

CONTENTS

Enigma Called Dislife: a Fable *1*

The Drum Major and the Governor *11*

The Execution of Aga Killam *25*

A Jackpot in April *53*

The Engineering Dean's Tale *87*

To Tangle with Tarzan *111*

A Song for the Parade *149*

The High Dim's Revenge *167*

Glossary of African Terms *219*

About the Author

Chudi Uwazurike, who was educated at the University of Nigeria, Nsukka, received higher degrees at Lagos and Harvard Universities. A winner of the 1975 USIS John F. Kennedy Essay Prize and the 1978 Nigerian Independence Essay Competition Award, his play, *House of Little Regrets* won First Prize at the Niger State Schools Drama Festival in 1980. Another play, *The Flycatcher's Identity* was performed off-Broadway in New York in 1991. He is the founder of the theater group, Nakanu Players of New York, and of *Profiles International*, a periodical on Africa and the world. His scholarly works have appeared in various journals in Europe, the United States, and Nigeria.

 ***Enigma Called Dislife:***

A Fable

The old man

rose and faced the assembly. Young and old, ugly and comely, whole and deformed, rich and poor, holy and profane, the men were all there, in the shade of the great Ugbaka tree at the village square, with its cascades of branches and leaves. They had gathered for some purpose, but that was not what now irked the old one. He had a thing or two to say in reply to some youth — a man of fifty and over, father of six, township type, employee of many, but still a youth — who had dared a speech on the nature of life, the wonders of the world of gold and dazzle beyond the backwoods of this land. He had spoken, his head high, his chin up, about the mysteries of a world greater than the Mbara vastness. But everyone knew he was but a pretender to the sober ranks of the few *nze-n'ozo*, who also live to join the *oji ofo* ancients, standing at a level only beneath that of the gods themselves.

The old man adjusted his toga-like *lappa*, cleared his throat and looked about and around him. The wind rustled the leaves above, the trees swayed, the grass stirred as the birds sang. The somewhat scraggly white hair that strode down his head to his jaw — ending in a half foot-long beard of sheer grey-white — seemed to join nature's animated song and dance. Suddenly he began to speak, leaning on his third leg, his great shining, walking stick that had been with him two dozen years.

"Life," he thundered. "I shall tell you about life, the story of life, this enigma called life." He cleared his throat and took a pain-filled arthritic step and cried out in a low voice the greeting

"*Umunna-kwenu!*" *People of my blood, unity.*

"Yaarh!" roared back the audience

"*Kwezue-nu!*" *Everyone now!*

"Yaarh!"

"Life! I shall tell you about life, for you are all but starry-eyed youngsters, most of you. You know less than your new ways pretend."

The men assembled there looked from one to the other: The old *nze* is at it again! It was said he had seen too much of the world. Why, it was said he had been to all eight corners of the earth. He had met red and brown nations; he had even been to strange schools and knew magic. Fond of talking like the ancestors themselves, the old man had a voice that rasped like a metal gong, loud enough to be heard by the women and children by the hearth preparing the evening meal.

Now he was calm, his expression betraying no change. He just stood there, like a sculpted offering to the gods; the only sign of movement was the wind rustling his beard and his toga. Gradually the hubbub died down. He cleared his voice; it sounded like the growl of a roiling sea wave. With a sweep of the air as he threw the loose end of his toga about him, he began to speak again, and this was the tale he recounted:

Life is a story told in countless moons, yet it began but on a certain day, when the sun had gone up high and early, and everywhere was of a sight wondrous to behold. Mighty Lion of the golden mane and frightful roar, he roamed the veld with his three cousins, Tiger, Wolf, and Hyena, rampaging like the real jungle lords they were born to be. Beneath the grass, Pythons, Cobras, and Vipers lay coiled at rest. Overhead, up in the air, the Eagle and the Heron, the Kite and the Crow, all diving and singing, extolled the unfettered freedom that was theirs to relish ever and evermore. Beneath the birds of the air, in that watery world of streams and rivers that fed the mighty Osimiri, the vast sea that circles the world, fishes of all shapes and sizes, from the mighty Whale and the sharp-toothed Shark to the tiny Starfish, all flapped their fins genuflecting in myriad ways, like shy little girls learning their Agbagwu festival steps. Yet others moved with the grace and ferocity of feathered arrows on the attack.

Life indeed! You also remember that each river has a bank. Now it is on the bank of one of these rivers that I shall tell you about life. About life! About what it comes to in the end. One day — and this was but one among many when the sun was at its zenith, and all nature was up and about, in search of shelter and rest — a lazy, large Alligator ambled forward from its lair by the riverside to the more open but shaded undergrowth, just by the sandy stretch of the river bank. It was high noon, as I said, and everyone was settling down for a nap. Nothing was to be seen stirring. Most were glad enough to keep away from the fire-darts of the Sun God, Anyanwu. Everyone now lay or sank leisurely, reclined, each at one with Mother Earth, Ani. As they lay there, all creatures of Heaven, at peace with their world, there was nothing to disturb them, nothing to suggest imminent calamity. They were a sight to behold! The Hedgehog and his six followers; the Housefly and his house-mate; the Soldier Ant, black and shiny, with his comrades; the White Termite and his brood; the Red-necked Lizard and his bevy of colorful females, the Grey Moth and company, the fat-cheeked, dotted-skin Toad and his clan. Male and female, young and old, whole and disabled, all were gathered there in the cool undergrowth, taking in the afternoon of this one day in the age of paradise.

Mark my words, and remember how it was then: They had all the world to themselves. There was no war and no covetousness, no greed and no envy. They had long since learnt to live in peace among themselves. And when the Lizard and the Frog eyed the Fly more than once, it was in friendly concern, not hungry lust. But having warred and fought for years on end, they had finally learnt to live and let others live. The youngsters played together, chased each other about, screaming with abandon and pleasure. The adults chatted in mild tones among themselves, listening to the essence of each word of wisdom from the wizened ones. In those days of yore, age meant everything — but that is another matter.

It was a world full of such contentment that when a big green Snake arrived, accompanied by a Millipede, a Centipede, an amphibious Eel and an Earthworm, for a conference on some matter of mutual interest to the world of Reptilia, no one took more than cursory notice of them. Those friendly enough with the new entrants merely exchanged felicitations, turning from one side to the other for greater comfort. Then came time to feast, and plenty there was to eat and be merry about, with musicians and dancers and acrobats everywhere venting the joy of life.

But appearances, as we know, may reveal only so much and no more. Everyone forgot, as day gave way to market cycles, these to the endless moons, as the land fed fat and made merry, no one remembered the prophecy. The one-legged Old Woman of the River, had she not warned of a terrible famine fated to swing by every now and then? There would always be the rainy day, the day when the unthinkable happens and the impossible becomes thinkable. Would it be today, tomorrow, this year, or the one after that? No one knew.

So then it came to pass, my people, that behind every evil is to be found some matter of doubt or dissension.

When the Lizard and the Toad eyed the Fly, for instance, was it not a pointer that, were it not for the live-and-let-live understanding in that world of the damp undergrowth, the wrong side of their natures might have pushed them to stick out their long tongues? But there — when you stop to think of it — is life not full of many such moves in endless succession, some swift like a Mamba on the strike, others so slow it is like the fixed regularity of time itself. But mark my words again, the Old Woman of the River was right. For no one took note of the Alligator, apparently asleep all the while. Though only his head was visible, his stomach was unusually flat; he had missed the feast! No one had thought to wake him up. Hunger, the father of greed and mother of evil....

Suddenly, his little eyes opened and his heart gladdened. He closed those squinting eyes again — but from his mouth, his long tongue flicked forth: This time he knew what was bound to happen without fail. And he went forth with his slumber, save that once in a while he created a minor earthquake as his tongue flicked inward. By the time it was over, the magic bird Nza was the only one left to sing the doleful song whose tunes many of today know so well. Of the meaning, however, they know nothing. The words of the song are these:

> Life is
> > like
>
> The open mouth
> Of the Alligator
> > steady
> > obscene
> > reeking
>
> Life is
> > like
>
> The Bee
> > buzzing
>
> Like the Fly
> > flapping greedy
> > sniffing ubiquitous
>
> Life is
> > like
>
> The Gecko
> > after
>
> The Fly
> > like
>
> The Serpent
> > after
>
> The Gecko

like
Nemesis
    after
Them all
    Us all ...

Life's like that
    A chain
Tail to head
    to toe
Running and
    rushing
    blind
    into
    the open mouth
    of the
    Alligator
    Soon to flap shut

To them darkness come, but
To us one more quake of destiny
    also named Dislife.

    The old man hobbled in a trot on his third leg and raised his oxtail wand of a thousand strands and saluted, "*Umunna Kwenu!*"
    "*Yaarh!*" came the response
    "*Kwezue-nu!*"
    "*Yaarh!*"
    "My people, words are proverbs and proverbs are metaphors. Listen well, so you may learn well. So said the ancients before me. I am done." He hobbled back to his spot, sat down, and reached for

his snuff box, leaving his meaning as vague as ever. Indeed the young green ones were more confused now. But the *nze-na-ozo* understood him well enough. They nodded and chuckled as the rest of the gathering looked around and about in great puzzlement.

 # The Drum Major and the Governor

The sun came

down on the sweating crowd mercilessly. Everywhere, a sea of heads, shifting and bobbing like so many flotsam on a seatide. Those in the thick of the throng could hardly turn anymore, and the heat from their neighbors not only stank, but seemed to sear. But what could one do? It was not every day that the Governor left the capital to honor remote provinces such as this. Who, which man in Issa, would be foolhardy enough to stay home when the Governor comes on a visit? See, even people from places far and wide, from the other hamlets, even from the nearby townships, would descend to see His Excellency make a stop at Issa, to wave to him, to savor the presence of power. Issa would be put on the map once and for all time, explained the school headmaster to the Chief.

But why has he not come yet? The Divisional Officer had pronounced most solemnly: The Governor (whom he said was his friend of old) would be in Issa Division at exactly noon that day, perhaps even before then, before the sun reached the center of the universe, its heat sizzling hot. He had told the elders and the Chief so. Everyone had been informed: the headmaster and the teachers, the pastors and priests, the post delivery man, the women's dancing groups, the big farmer for whom everyone else worked, Chief Uka Onyeuberu. They all had been told, anyone who counted for anything in Issa, when to expect the Governor: twelve noon — at the latest. So everyone had been there since nine or ten, some even earlier.

But now, it was twelve and past, in fact, twelve-thirty, and there was no sign of the Governor still. Fifteen minutes came and went, then twenty, thirty, forty minutes.

A thousand eyes and more stood transfixed on the lone tarred road that ran past the somewhat insignificant headquarters of the Issa Division. Among them was young Azu Amaku, who had risen with the early morning moon for a trip to the stream. A thousand eyes and more, necks craning, they waited the coming of His Excellency the Governor, eyes fixed toward the great shimmering highway from which the powerful personage would come. Since the past week when the news of the Governor's coming started whirling in the air, the jarred roadway had been thrown into one bit again. No one had been sure at first he was coming. But all of a sudden everyone knew it was for real. Overnight the road that led to the capital from the distant city past Issa took on a new appearance, something almost worthy of admiration. Everyone hoped the road could stay that way for a few weeks more — that would be lucky. Last time a most important personage had chanced by, the Ministry of Works people had come bedraggling themselves to close up the myriad potholes — no mean work on the whole. But the accursed holes had barely lasted a week. They had broken up in open blisters baring a

The Drum Major and the Governor

blood-curdling mix of red earth and black macadam once the rains came.

People had merely glared at the mess but otherwise said nothing. What could one say, to whom did one protest when the High Council was in Lagos, and the goateed excellency had made clear he was answerable to no one but the armed junta in Lagos? The few car owners of Issa, with their slightly louder voices, eventually ceased to complain when they realized no one was listening, let alone about to do anything. Everyone soon got used to crawling at snail speed, though many an impatient man would once in a while attempt faster motion than caution held reasonable. Things invariably often ended in woeful tales to tell, of broken shafts and head-on collisions with the cars thrown off-course because of a failed brake or something.

But now that hardly mattered anymore. The potholes had been closed up again — this was hardly the time for ill-will now with the visit of the Governor. At long, long last he was coming! Though everyone knew that were it to be in the legendary Era of Clean Vote, the man might never have smelt any House of the Elect his whole life, it still did not matter now. The mere closure of those dismal potholes that had kept reminding everyone that the country only recently passed through difficult times was enough to keep them sweating in the sun, waiting for his arrival. For everyone knew, too, that it was sure to be the start of a new chapter. A scholarship scheme, for sure, would be unfolded; perhaps a new hospital, perhaps some factory or other; something, for sure. To boot, a new paramount chief might be proclaimed for the province — the Eze whom everyone would hail Ikem Issa would be in the lead. Chieftains, many self-proclaimed, were the rage of the age.

A sea of heads, large and small, was all young Azu could make out. To the journalists present, this was a dilemma. For how could anyone hazard a guess as to how that might be reliable? Least of all, to the census experts and the newspaper people, for whom hundreds could become thousands; a sea of heads belonged to the realm of the unfathomable. The reporter from the *Daily Renaissance* was a rather reflective type. As he explained to the young features cub from the state TV network, it all depends on which way the winds turned the center of things! Should the entire lot in government be kicked out tomorrow, the editors would order a new track overnight to revise all past estimates. But for the record, here, as far as the eye could see — it was good to be on the safe side — was an ocean of dark glistening heads, all eager for His Excellency's arrival.

Standing there in the lead, his drum major's baton held out, the tipped end on the ground, the rest of the school band behind him, Azu was the envy of his fellows. He was the school's drum major. For him it had been a long week indeed. He was ready to fling and swing his baton, raise it with both hands above his head, then hold it now on the left hand, out front shoulder high, now to the right, shoulder high, outstretched. He had long mastered the intricate art of twisting the long black and white drum major's baton between his fingers, underneath his legs, from one pair of fingers on one hand to the other. Azu had long become used to the wonder and the cheering of the other school children each October 1st, Independence Anniversary Celebration Day, as the Issa village school band strutted about the green-grey grass of the soccer field. They were all boys — but they knew the girls giggling by the sidelines would be waiting to make jokes.

Now the Elementary Standard Six youth stood at ease, one hand holding forth the ribboned baton like a decorated spear, the sun's heat swirling all about and through his white hat, through his thick but worn red-and-white uniform. His was the only proper uniform. Why, he even wore canvas shoes; the other boys in the twelve-piece marching band were dressed in their whites and sandals. A third of the group thought themselves lucky to be wearing cut-outs sown by the village shoemaker from discarded Goodyear rubber tires. Azu remembered now how he had risen early, his brother still snoring on the bamboo bed they shared, and prepared to leave for the stream. It had been somewhat dark as he opened the door to his hut and walked into the compound.

"Is that you, Azu?"

He rubbed his eyes and was astonished to see his father and mother were already awake. She was setting about for breakfast, readying for his big day. His father, he noticed in even greater astonishment, was himself cleaning his drum major's uniform and his canvas shoes. Azu had forgotten to do it yesterday after the bandmaster gave it out to them from the school store. They had practiced all day long, and he had fallen asleep by the fire after the evening meal of cocoyam porridge.

Azu sensed, without his father fully saying so, that he half-expected some miracle or other to occur. He had spoken of how great men gave scholarships to secondary schools, of why it was important his son summon his talent's greatest possibility, be at his best this day, for it could be his passport to the big cities and the world beyond this luckless corner of the earth. His eyes lit up as he looked expectantly at the dais above which a somewhat worn rainbow-colored tarpaulin hung against the sun's heat. He shook his head, wondering if he would ever get to sit there when he grew up to be a man. He noted well enough how only a few men tend to sit up there again and again. They were already seated, those whom everyone knew were the truly important ones of Issa.

There was the new Eze, the high chief whose title of Ikem Issa bespoke of its ancient martial origin, whose right to the chair was in sharp dispute; with the Chieftaincy Tribunal failing to resolve anything, the matter had since been referred to the Governor himself. He sat, a crown in the form of an eagle-feathered hat trimmed with gold, adorning his head, his face contorted with the wrinkles of worry. He sat, the Eze, surrounded by other lesser chiefs, some of his own creation. They were now all over the place. You could hear many grumble out loud: These chieftains with their many titles and blood feuds, will be the unmaking of the fiercely republican Igbo. A cynic, seeing the popularity of the rush for status once suggested it was about time each family had a chief this and a chief that, in keeping with the need for even-handedness! But that was for eggheads to mumble. Everyone else saw the great possibilities in all this. Divisional Officer N. D. Ibezim was seated to the Eze's right, near the man's younger wife, who usually came to such occasions with him. The D. O.'s wife was also with him, seated to his left. Uka Onyeuberu equally had a seat next to the dais where the Governor would stand to speak. It was a great honor, though many people whispered openly that Onyeuberu was as dubious as his undisguised opulence. Then came the headmaster and the second head, those two who never agreed on a single thing between them, not even on the nature of the three R's. The postmaster was given a seat behind the Catholic parish priest who sat next to the Anglican pastor. The rest reasonably left the two men of God to themselves, sure they would soon be lamenting over the falling standard of Christianity in Issa, the growth of "heathenism," and the challenge of girls who no longer paid Easter dues to the catechist nor made any charity visits to the needy, the sick, and the bereaved.

    The D. O., an early Ibadan graduate in the classics, had asked that both men be kept together near enough to him, for he would not rule out the possibility of the two disagreeing on a point outside the Bible. For, in addition, they represented two poles in the land, north and south, in the tussle for the chieftaincy, with people of the downstream in one camp, those of the other end placing their fate in a separate basket. That was one way to keep one's ears to the ground, wasn't it? Ibezim was a man with a mischievous bent who considered himself a professional with a job to do. So, even as he chatted occasionally with the Eze, he strained an ear in the other direction, though thus far with little success. Both men of divine calling knew their limits; they dwelt instead on the fierce weather and the coming of the next farming season.

Somewhere in the crowd, the journalist wiped his brow with an already wet handkerchief; his colleague was fiddling with his pen and papers, though he felt only God knew what on earth he found to write about this desolate place; but he knew the editor would excoriate his urban bias and lacking of sensitivity in not nosing out news from apparent nothingness. What would make the most sense — the patience of the school children who had lined up since seven that morning or the brightly-clad leaders of the land in their elevation? But would that be "news?" Involuntarily he lifted his face to the road on either side of which stood the little things in their fading red-upon-white uniforms, sweating from head to toe and shielding their eyes against the sun while straining their necks at the slightest sound of an approaching vehicle. Each time they were reduced to witnessing no more than a lorry or two carrying market mamas, baskets of foods strapped atop their heads, or a minibus with a strap-hanging conductor crying needlessly for passengers, given the state of his already overcrowded van. Once in a while a real pleasure car cruised by, and necks would truly crane forward, only to draw back at the sight of an upraised cane. "When the Governor comes near, we shall know, surely children, don't worry," the buxom mistress in blue full-length dress reassured the pupils in a distant voice.

"How shall we know?" two or three tiny voices quipped. The lady glared at them through her round glasses, making them lower their heads. It had been drummed into everyone's head back at school, had it not, never to talk but to wave to the Governor, at most to be seen, not heard, to simply and loudly chant in sonorous repetition: "Welcome to Issa, Oh, welcome, Your Excellency!" Nothing more than that. Good manners, obedience, discipline — there is nothing greater. The mistress, uttering nary a word, spoke only with her eyes. Nevertheless she deigned an answer: "The sirens — you don't know what they are — they will be squawking, singing like the scoutmaster's whistle or a strong wind hurrying through the branches!" She had thought of saying squealing like a pig in pain but changed her mind.

The children nodded understanding, erect in their nervous expectation. Everything would soon come to pass, they knew, for it would be in this field that the Governor would enter to talk to the people, from where he would walk to declare open the new police post some three hundred yards away, though the D. O. feared he might like to go in a car if he got to know the place was farther than a fraction of a mile. But then there was no motorable way as such.

So, as the sun grew higher and higher, and stronger, too, the time went on past one, past two towards three. People began to think of the midday meal as stomachs growled and many sought out tree shades: Having tired of standing, the elders took to a corner to scoop their brown snuff or chew tobacco leaves to clear their sun-drenched heads.

Just then the droning sound of a heavy vehicle came whirling out of nowhere. Presently a huge black lorry-like bus came up along the mainroad at full speed, but soon slowed down and made for the new police post; it was filled and brimming with soldiers.

"The Governor!" cried the *Daily Renaissance* man, and soon the news was everywhere. Soon also another news item was in the air: that what had been holding up the Governor all along was the collapse of one of the numerous culverts dotting the highway in place of real bridges: The army field engineers in the convoy had hopped down to take a look and knew at once the poor thing could not stand a ton more. This lorry had only minutes earlier made it across, the rest of the party on the other side. The men had been asked to go on ahead to see how things stood before the Governor arrived. While a hasty crowd of the usually ragged workmen were quickly assembled to put up some repair, the Governor had sat in his air-conditioned car sipping cold beer and flitting through a newspaper. He even toyed with the idea of calling off the visit entirely but was prevailed upon to have some patience.

His passage — now so imminent — was for the people of Issa, a moment of destiny. The Governor was within earshot! He was in the land! The crowd was already joyfully restive; the school children on the alert, dusting themselves, wiping their tired faces, and smoothing their crumpled uniforms — quite under the stern eyes of the mistress and the masters; many had reappeared from thin air, as it were, craning forward again.

A few unruly schoolboys, herded by the lean-faced, uncompromising tutors, were resisting being pressed back into the lines. The Brass Band boys had taken the field just in front of the dais and were rehearsing lightly the first stanza of the National Anthem,

Nigeria we hail thee
   our own dear native land
   though tribe and tongue may differ
   in brotherhood we stand....

The headmaster hurriedly came down from the dais, inspected the boys, approved, then hurried back to where the chiefs and the rest sat to take his own seat. He must be seen among his ilk. Other sons of Issa, home and abroad, of any weight, had also gone over to the chief and the D. O. to stand behind them, so that when the time came, they would all be properly introduced as having contributed one way or the other to make Issa what it was today. The headmaster would read the marathon address on behalf of the unlettered Eze; the D. O. feared the Governor may not have the inclination to listen to the dozen pages, although with any luck his secretary should be around to accept a copy. He knew that like all the rest, the address would plead for everything under the sun: a clinic, a secondary school, running water, better roads, appointment of a son of the soil to the cabinet, perhaps a telephone line, maybe an educational television set, and a library to boot, whatever else may enter the needs of these demanding people.

Suddenly the noise froze. The siren came again and again — clearly, continuously, ringing. A row of outriders came into view; army jeeps, flashy cars — the longest line ever seen by Azu Amaku and his friends. The school children began to wave: "Welcome to Issa, Your Excellency! Welcome to Issa, O, Excellency! Welcome, welcome!"

They were still chanting their welcome as the fleet of cars passed on. The windows of the large silver-grey Citroen opened and His Excellency waved briefly. The fleet kept on moving. The

Governor had a pressing engagement back in the capital city; a dignitary from Lagos was due. The delay at the river had cost Issa the minutes allotted for His Portly Excellency to take a look at the headquarters and for his people to ensure his picture hung in the right place next to that of the head of state.

The cars disappeared down the hill, the rear brought up by yet another truck filled with soldiers. The men on the dais half-stood up, agape. The drum major for once felt his fingers miss the baton. It flew in the air and came crashing down with a soft clatter on the tired green-grey grass of the soccer field. The younger Amaku looked up into the crowd searching for his father.

 # The Execution of Aga Killam

Now, as far as

the eye could see, the Bar Beach bristled with people — a mammoth crowd that bore testimony to the great interest roused by sustained media reports concerning the next "Bar Beach Show." The criminal Aga Killam was going at last to the stakes; society could be rid of one more venom, with immediate effect, thanks to the determined men who spoke of law and order and discipline.

As usual, excited crowds were there ahead of the officials. The sun blazed down haughtily on them, the fine bright brown sand of the beach taking in dripping sweat. The sea before them rose and rolled in vast waves, washing the place but hardly sending any cooling draughts. The usual throng of bathers and sun-tanners had been asked to leave the limits of the whizzing bullets that might — doubt it not — miss their man that wide. There were no boats to be seen even in the far distance, and the great ships calling from across the world beyond had been asked to sail off in the meantime.

It would not be the first execution of criminals by the authorities. Why, the sands first soaked criminal blood nearly two decades ago and, on the average, every six months since then. They were brought to Bar Beach and went down in their own blood, crimson payment for the mayhem they wrought in their wake — even those who had drawn no blood. But then, what was the difference, argued the Prosecutor-General? Threatening to take blood was, in cases of armed robbery, as good as having taken it anyway. Once in a while, as when fourteen sagging peasants were mowed down at one go, an argument had gone round and about in *The Times of Lagos* about all this being inhuman and uncivilized and all that. There had been little said of the victims nor of the right of the authorities to punish crime. They got nowhere, given the wave of bloody crimes and the dread they caused law-abiding men and women. Thankfully something was being done. The wooden stakes were already set. What was holding up the show? The crowd was thirsty enough for revenge, their growling for it rising.

-II-

The two journalists entered the Volkswagen. One turned the key, and the old engine revved. The car swept out of the narrow Kakawa Street and on to the double-laned Marina. They were heading towards the Bar Beach.

One was a rather small man who laughed a great deal; his partner was, in contrast, reticent in speech and in emotion. But they were good enough friends, always preferring to go after assignments together whenever the chance came. The small one was called Madu; the other went by the name of Dele.

"Say, Dele, have you got the tape with you?"

"What for?"

"Background noises — must get that too."

"What for? We are not broadcasters," protested Dele.

"Fans the imagination — presents a more complete mental picture as one knocks out the story."

"Okay, but aren't we trained to use our eyes, Madu, not just our ears?"

"Shut up, silly," growled Madu. "I got better eyes than you. Deny that and quench! For one, you use these double-layered eye-glasses, and I don't."

"Whatever you say!" Dele yawned a little.

As usual there was a traffic go-slow along the Marina. A policeman wearing a blue shirt, khaki trousers, and white-peaked cap stood at a road intersection, his hands moving almost mechanically as he directed the traffic in four directions.

As usual people milled in a throng, hurrying in and out of the huge office blocks lining the Marina. The endemic workmen were around too, unearthing, filling, refilling, repairing. A common sight of the Marina, they shared this distinction with the beggars who stood astride the walls and the trees, in dazed misery, the few brown Kobo coins disfiguring their aluminum bowls, all they had to show for the day-long chanting pleas. It was said they were often locked in mutual antagonism with the other mendicants of a sort, the wristwatch and the condiments hawkers who shoved their articles at passers-by, pleading for a purchase, distracting them from the pangs of conscience that might have made a few more dig deeper into their pockets of good will. So Madu had once described this side-struggle for survival in a news report on the growing wave of beggarliness.

The two journalists passed the traffic policeman and climbed the road that passed by the Senior Officers' Mess and the Bonny

Camp of the army. Just then something seemed to snap in Dele's mind.

"Madu!"

"What now?" The edge in Dele's tone startled Madu a little.

"Do you know I am not happy?"

"Not by a mile. What's the matter?"

"This thing today."

"The execution?"

"Yes. Ever since the judgment — "

Madu shrugged. "You must remember we are under a military dictatorship."

"No Nigerian journalist needs lessons on that, man. But remember this too. One must not, because wars involve horrors, refuse to go on the offense if necessary, to leave what must be done, undone."

"That aphorism is too philosophical to be of much use," Madu began slowly. "Under military rule, a tiny minority of trained killers are armed; others, the majority, are not. The strangest reality, the taxpayer's guns turned on him by his paid guards! We exist in a state of animation, fearful suspense, hovering overhead like Democle's sabre. It's not as if one is afraid of freedom, press or personal, or that it's not worth fighting for. It's just that — freedom to ask questions under dictatorships at times is an unaffordable luxury...."

"The ostrich hypothesis, I call this!" laughed Dele. Having known Madu for so long, he could not remember when last his friend had had to speak in this deliberate tone, summing up his views in a slow, long-winded manner. "Spare me the civics," he muttered, "though I know you may very well be right."

They had been assigned to what at first had appeared a commonplace trial of an armed robber who had carried out a series of daring raids at the expense of highly placed citizens of the land and had been caught in the long run. They had filed a number of widely read stories on the matter. But for some reason, this had not been a typical open-and-shut case. At times they had thought they smelt fish; at times, inconsistencies. But always they believed there were certain open-ended questions in search of answers.

"The fight for press freedom most continue, I tell you, and in earnest too," Dele was saying. "And we the practitioners in the field must show the initiative, take the lead."

"That's right," murmured the other. "Perhaps then we may get our own bullets, and there will be no news to be posted."

"You are rather pessimistic."

"Realistic is more apt."

"Publish the truth and be damned, remember."

"Where truth is appreciated."

"Truth is truth — regardless of the cowardice of any age."

"But appreciation is critical to productivity," said Madu, still concentrating on the road. "What do you do in a land that cheers only when it's safe but slinks away, tail between legs, when the fat-one-with-the-M-gun appears to take you away?" He was dying for a cigarette. That was the one thing he shared most in common with Dele. The latter lit one, took a draw, blew the smoke at him, making the car swerve a little — then graciously stuck it into his mouth for him.

"Thanks," grunted Madu.

"I am interested in what you imply by appreciation and the lack of it." Dele drew him back.

"People look at your name and not at your face to know if and why you are telling the truth."

"So what's wrong with that? Shouldn't people know who is

telling them what and react accordingly? Do they have the choice of getting close enough to scrutinize the face of the source? What really are you saying?"

"That truth is relative."

"A case then of beauty in the eye of the beholder?"

"Of Stout Beer, bitter to some, tasty to others."

"Truth is truth. It will rise on its own, it will stand the test of time. Publish it."

"And be damned by whipping and a shaven head for your troubles?"

"But be canonized by history."

"In the some far-off future?"

"Now and ever more. Everyday history is made. Nigerians never forget, believe me."

"You are dreaming. Our memories here are too short."

Involved in their typical high-flown banter, the two reporters sped on to the scene of the execution. Along the way, somewhere in Victoria Island, they ran into a convoy of military vehicles. Among them was a big black van preceded by an armored car. Behind came three jeeps and two lorry-loads of soldiers with their weapons glinting in the dying sun. Could that be the execution party?

Dele remembered something else that made the other almost come to screeching halt right at the entry to one of those concrete bridges the world denizens of Lagos immediately branded "fly-overs." "Dr. Ebi's note!" he cried, full of the flush of sudden recall. "Remember Comrade Mansfrend Ebi's threat?"

Madu betrayed more than a hint of the emotion of the self-conscious intellectual journalist he always took himself to be. "No wonder!" he cried in return, managing to keep the car from veering into the other lane. "I thought it was all a little too fishy being escorted to one's death by the elite guards of the nation in this fashion."

For the armed men in the convoy belonged to the commando unit whose insignia was the skull and the shrapnel.

-III -

Boundary. Odd name, but fit for the spot where the rest of Lagos met and parted with the widely feared Ajegunle district. Here the grand buses stopped, disgorged their passengers and circled round back toward the city. What a sight the droning buses were to behold: some long and elegant in their blood-red colors, others dour and somber in their grey, each with a crew of two beside the driver, hollering and giving the heave-ho like the great ships at the wharves.

The young man in the torn shirt stood waiting in the milling crowd. He would have preferred a *molue* minibus, but only the huge, creaking, dirty lorrylike *bolekajas* buses surrounded the place now. Every single one that came was already too crowded. Occasionally, one got a bus that was going all the way to Eko, the Old City, from here, but the surer bet was Oyingbo. Perhaps he was waiting at the wrong place and ought to move up a little. The ground was slippery with dark mud; the stench from the uncollected refuse and from the cattle abattoir along Malu road enveloped the whole atmosphere. People bumped into one another and cursed and laughed in turns. If one looked closely at the faces of the younger men in the crowd, there was discernible a certain element of both hope and despair written in bold relief, which just about summed up the situation.

Lewa Akandu was not in the mood for any reflections now. His whole mind was there, far away at Bar Beach. He still felt angry with himself for having slept so long. He looked at the dimming sun and felt like sinking down. Suppose he missed the last minutes on earth of his brother? Not that he was to blame for not waking early enough; it would have been worse if he had not slept at all. He had spent the whole of yesterday and the night with Agaranta Akandu — his older brother whom the world had come to know as Aga Killam but whom he knew was not that other Aga Killam the entire city of Lagos seemed to dread. True Agaranta had been with the wrong types. Why he had even done a thing or two no one should be proud of, but it was not he who had held members of the Club Delite hostage for an hour and broken the leg of Chief J. B. C. Inglisman after seizing a hoard of gold chains and watches and wads of crisp currency. But the Armed Robbery Tribunal, sitting in secret, had allowed no appeals — not that it mattered, since he couldn't have afforded a lawyer anyway. Nor had it been easy to see the condemned man. Lewa had finally greased his way through the maximum security prison fat cats to allow him his guaranteed legal right as next of kin.... He had sat in his brother's dreary death cell, struggling not to choke. While he had prayed for his soul, Aga had gone on with his humming — not in sorrow, not in anger — just the way a man out on an evening walk might whistle old airs. At times he would come over and ask him not to mind, not to abandon their aged mother, to ensure her heart did not break, to reassure her he was innocent of the charges, that he had led a better life between Maroko and Ajegunle than his killers would claim, that he would surely come back in reincarnation, making sure his name was not lost.

    Such bravado as Aga put on had not prevented the tears from rolling down his cheeks and mouth and dripping down to mingle with his brother's sweat to form a sultry pool on the cold floor of the dismal cell. This, indeed, was the end, the end of a thousand-mile journey from the farthest interior where Lagos had been sung of in fables and wonderment. He had learnt the carpenter's trade, and

Lewa had become an itinerant tailor. But Aga was not the sort to live the humble carpenter's life. With decent jobs scarce and stomachs hungry, there were other things to do, to get into, to make ends meet, for those with the energy and the mind.

A bus finally came, slowing down but not fully stopping. Lewa caught hold of the handle and made a swing up. He need not have worried. The surging crowd behind was enough to sweep him off his feet and into the bus. But he could not get a seat and had to stand. Not that he particularly cared. In fact, it meant nothing to him. His most nagging preoccupation now was to hope that the Bar Beach bullets didn't ring out before he arrived. Aga had pleaded with him to tell nothing to their mother — though they both knew well enough their mother would drop right dead the moment she heard of the killing of her oldest son, the leading light who had gone off to the cities, to the new proving ground of the land, who had left long ago with assurances he would some day come riding home, laden with his share of the good life. Lewa promised himself to stop recalling this.

Wedged in between folds of flesh, Lewa thought about how final these things could be! He now recalled with some bitterness what the Jamantha Boys had hinted they planned to do; their name came from a hero of the Indian magic films they watched at Chekwas Cinema every afternoon. An accomplished swordsman endowed both with irresistible charm with the ladies and a great voice that would roar "Jamantha!" as he plunged his sword through evil enemies, younger boys often could be found practicing with wooden swords and yelping "Ja-maaa-ntha!" But what of their swagger, their oath to rescue Agarantha? Lewa bit his lip at the teasing foolishness of Aga's boastful friends — not to speak of the cruelty of toying with the impossible. But, of course, they wouldn't dare. The two brothers dismissed the Jamantha crowd as being no more than up to their usual bluff and loud talk.

-IV-

His Excellency, Military Governor Oremu, finished signing the heap of papers and threw his weighty frame back on the sofa chair and yawned. It had been a hard day's work. He patted rather than scratched his balding temple, yawned again, then looked down at his bulging stomach. Must cut down, you know, or risk obesity. Wasn't that what the doctor had termed the disaster?

Semba Oremu was in service uniform — khaki-green fatigues with bright gold-colored epaulets, the insignia of a colonel's rank on his shoulders. Before him, on a silver-rimmed shield atop the huge obeche table, stood the colors of the brigade from which he had been appointed, imprinted with the skull and the shrapnel of the thousand warriors. Nicknamed the Winged Death Brigade from their civil war exploits, his was the most famous unit. He had been part of the liberation of Port Harcourt.

It was a spacious office. Befitting was the word. The wide glass windows let in enough light through the soft lacy curtains. Above hung a chandelier, meant to be of use once night came. But the lights that came from its many filaments now seemed merely decorative. Colonel Oremu usually thought of himself as a child of light and hated the idea of shutting off signs of daylight on the pretext that electricity was more than enough.... The walls were painted light blue. On them, in various positions, hung almanacs and paintings of military life and events. One was a photograph of midranking officers taken during his days at the Staff Officers Training School at Mons in Britain. Another was of him commanding men of the Winged Death in a desperate attack during the war fought to "Go on with one Nigeria — A task that must be accomplished!" How odd they sound these days, those slogans of war! Both were the two images he would always instinctively turn towards whenever the mood took him.

Loyalty, honor, duty. Why, he still held and would always hold onto the officer-and-gentleman ideals infused in those foreign academies. He had read with disgust Dr. Mansfrend Ebi's diatribe about how men trained to kill and maim are really not meant to govern! But he wasn't paying attention to that communist anymore. He was a rather busy man with a lengthy list of private and official engagements. Often when he thought of the old politicians whom Nzeogwu and the other officers and other ranks from all over the federation had driven from office in '66, he tended to pity them. Perhaps it was not all their fault. One could go insane in Nigeria as a public figure.

Yes, public figure. Once he had viewed that coinage with suspicion and distaste. Mere opportunism. But as Military Governor, it was different. Though not elected by the people, but here at the behest of a cabal of a dozen fellow-travellers, circumstances threw one up into public office, and the rest became unavoidable, yes, inevitable. People, smiling ear-to-ear, promptly cast you in the mould of the man of the hour, despite one's reservations, often half-hearted in its own right. The starched uniform, the silver-tipped swagger-stick, the shining black boots — they guaranteed that. The Central Command was aware of the potential for abuse. In fact, they had been instructed to avoid traces of inviting, "nice man" smiles in their official undertakings that might be misconstrued for unprofessional ends. Talented manipulators could read into their all-too-human visage — even from the official photographs alone. Oh, yes, Colonel Oremu ruminated as he examined a piece of communication from Kaduna, soldiers in power are not politicians. No, they are not, yes.

He looked at the official framed photograph of him. It was clearly the most dominant single item in His Excellency's office, looking down from above on the wall behind him and facing the door. The almost brooding military visage scowled at the nervous visitor, increasing the unease of those who also knew they were in the presence of a man with arms on his hips and in his drawers.

He had grown to love the decor of this office. Bose Ladi, the woman who acted as office manager — Oh, yes, there was such a post even in these parts — really had taste. The rugged floor, the double sofa by the end of the left wall, the flower pots with their sweet-smelling hibiscuses and periwinkles! She even contrived a little electrically operated fountain that played in a lighted glass enclosure, sending silvery rays that were a delight to behold.

The sofa in particular. He smiled to himself as he contemplated it for a moment. A most thoughtful, multi-purpose piece of furniture, this! Another trace of a smile appeared and disappeared instantly. He could hear machines clattering as Bebe typed out something. Must be on that matter of disgruntled elements trying to revive partisan politics when the emergency was still on and the ban had not been lifted. He made to press the button to summon her. Just then he heard the thudding of military boots along the passage. Only authorized people came this way. Must be his batman with the usual information about some trivial delegation wishing to see him on some silly issue. He was not a politician, they ought to know that, just a simple soldier. They ought to know that, though he had heard talk of people from his home district speaking of him becoming leader in the days ahead.

The doors opened, boots clicked, and a right arm shot out in smart salute. The young staff sergeant stood in stiff attention, praiseworthy in his starched kakhi and polished black boots.

"Sir! You asked me to remind you, sir!"

The colonel swung slightly on the swivel chair to face him, his favorite among the lot who worked here, and he made no secret of the fact. "How are you, Palu?"

The Execution of Aga Killam 39

"Fine, sir." The corporal still did not feel free with him, Oremu knew; in any case he must not be encouraged too far. "What is it?"

"The execution at Bar Beach."

Colonel Oremu gave an involuntary start, his face contorting. "I see. Oh, yes, yes, ah, yes. Okay, you may go now." He had not intended to dismiss Corporal Palu Ambama so quickly. Nor had he paid attention as the soldier clicked his boots again, saluted, and marched out of the room. Yes, he had almost forgotten about that young fool who deliberately threw his own life away for nothing in particular. The audacity of taking the Club Delite single-handedly, robbing those captains of industry and the professions, mouthing nonsense about rich and poor, breaking Chief Inglisman's arm so brazenly! The public was scandalized, the press stunned, and the Anti-Robbery Tribunal of which he was chairman, most furious. On reaching his desk, he had swiftly signed the warrant, as he had signed several others before, but this time gritting his yellowing teeth quite tightly. If the country is to run the way it should, criminals must be flushed out and severely dealt with accordingly. Some people were, to be sure, against the death penalty in principle and had offered verbose diatribes against it in the papers. Most of them were communists anyway.

But it was the attacks against this particular case of Aga Killam that irked him the most. Students had demonstrated and all kinds of threats and ultimatums surreptitiously thrown at the Governor. Appeals for clemency had been sent to him and published in the press. He could never understand the ambiguities of that entity called the public. How someone could possibly argue that this could be the wrong man, that he may not be the same Aga Killam they, the public, claimed for so long to have lived in dread of. Most puzzling was the threat by someone calling himself the real Aga Killam who vowed to pull a few surprises that would set Lagos on its ears. But the colonel knew well enough that with civilians talk was the cheapest commodity. He knew Dr. Mansfrend Ebi was as usual behind it. One of these days, that loud-mouth would get hauled off to Kirikiri and not all his friends overseas in Russia and in the Amnesty International could help get him out in one piece. Military boys in power are neither professors nor politicians; they settle anything they considered a nuisance by shutting up the loudest mouths, with trained despatch!

He rose to his full height, his whole bulk in tow, and ambled to where his cap hung. He stared at himself in the mirror by the corner, still frowning. Too big — but, yes, he looked good. In a huff he left for the room where the wide-screened television set had been installed.

Yes, he would personally watch the execution.

-V-

Chief Uzzi Elo came out of the Mercedes whose door was held open by the uniformed chauffeur and hurried towards the house. A flowered path led to the big doorway; but he was not indulging his usual habit of picking up the blooming flowers and sniffing them, a lingering love of scented flowers acquired from his boyhood days as a ward of some Catholic missionaries. Now the hour has come, and the course of justice must take its toll. The young man who had so humbled him would now weep his last; he must see him do so even on telly. He could still recall with deep embarrassment how everyone had been made to undress, how the rest of the doomed big wigs and their women could barely contain the sniggering at his massive torso and tiny underwear.

Uzzi Elo carried his bulky form with a certain grace. Not so tall, but fleshy, he had a jaunty walk and a passion for loud talk, though that awful hour in the ballroom of the Club Delite had dimmed his confidence in his ability to handle any situation any time, as he had long believed himself capable of. Even then he maintained a sartorial taste in European double-breasted and continental suits that hinted of the more fashionable clothiers of Paris and London. Alone among his full-bodied peers, he never got used to the agbada. This evening he was dressed in a dark suit with matching jet-black shoes, impressive to any beholder, awesome to the outgoing who graced Club Delite events in their gorgeous *aso oke* and large sunglasses.

The door swung open at his approach. He could hear the Mercedes being driven into the garage. He had told the chauffeur he wouldn't be going out again this evening; he had spent much of the day at the Federal Palace with a group of Swedes who were in the country on business.

The porter drew the glass door open for him, and he stepped into the ornate receiving room, where less consequential visitors would wait for him. The rug on the floor here was thin, but the seats were polished to shine. Photographs of him in various circumstances were placed at positions of great visibility. The flowered red and white curtains added to the special effect of the lavishly painted room to present an aura that never failed to strike.

Uzzi Elo strode through his grand living room. He was not entering the adjoining one separated by thick beds of curtains, which was smaller and much more to his taste, where he received special visitors. The family liked to call it the Whispering Room. He was going upstairs — not to the first floor, where the children had their suites; nor to the second, where the two wives still fought each other in eyetails, a state of affairs to which he paid little attention. He was going to the third, where alone to himself he could contemplate the world, a world at his beck and call.

There was still the matter of the threat to puzzle over...

On finally getting to the third floor and flopping onto the settee, he was thinking amid his gasps for air that it was time he installed a lift in the place — too winding and too far, this staircase. Tired him out each day; but only a little. Sure, of course, like every good doctor, his had spoken of the need for watching his consumption of venison and alcohol. He had also made mention of the need to avoid tension-inducing activities. But what with things to do at every turn! His personal opinion of life was that one needed a large dose of aggression to survive, and that was the way he had built himself almost from scratch. If the doctors thought that that was bad for his health, he personally knew that was a lot of good for his goals, his next moves...

He pressed one of those new-fangled, hand-held gadgets, and the telly came on. They had not yet begun showing the "Bar Beach Show," as people called the periodic executions. A group of fleshy wrestlers somewhere in America were exhibiting more boxing than wrestling techniques. He watched them awhile, wondering if these people had no other way to make money, real money. Each time one of the men hurled the other in mid-air and brought him crashing onto the canvas or when the one would seek to wrench off the arm of the other from its sockets, he found himself wincing. Then he took up the day's newspaper. Predictably, there were front-page write-ups on the execution and on the fact that the outrage had been committed as he, Chief Uzzi Elo, had been about to pop open a celebratory champagne bottle after his speech at the Club Delite's Annual Dinner, the premier social event in all the land.

It was a large living room with settees set around. The telly formed part of it. The rug here was about four inches deep and soft;

the glass-topped mahogany table in the center held a water-enclosed creature that changed color every few minutes; perhaps he would find a pair of little fishes to swim around it and complete the reconstruction of sea life. Overhead hung the chandeliers linked to a series of small and large balloons that ringed the room. He detested wallpapering or any disfiguring of the walls of his private apartments. He preferred the paint, oil paint, like the silvery types he had seen in Amsterdam. Apart from a life-size photograph of him and his two wives dancing during his chieftaincy installation, him wearing the traditional toga and a broad hat festooned with feathers and leaves and long fat beads, his wives resplendent in their head-gear, their lovely necks and fingers bedecked in pure gold, there was hardly much else by way of pictures. But there was the huge oil painting of him voluntarily executed and donated to him by an artist in search of instant renown — though even he recognized it as a caricature. Nevertheless as an act of magnanimity, though his enemies spoke of publicity-seeking, he had organized a press luncheon during which gifts had been presented, and he had donated a couple of thousands to the young talent, sending the starving sycophant into a paroxysm of gratitude. The event had duly appeared in the press — with some of his employees sending in praises to the "Letters to the Editor" section of the newspapers.

The sing-song push bell announced the presence of someone at the door. No one ever entered his apartment in his absence; when he was in, no one could easily saunter in. You only came when summoned. He rose and opened the door. It was his second wife, a woman in her late thirties; he should have known.

"Uzzi," she said simply, walking in.

"Ella?" He was concerned. There was something downcast about her. "Come in, odozi-aku. What's the matter?" Odozi-aku, arranger-of-the-family-wealth, a praise-name for wives who were not spendthrifts.

Ella winced at that but still turned on him with feigned surprise. "Who said anything was the matter?"

"Oh, come off it, dear! I can read your face like I was a fortune-teller!" Placing his arm on her neck he led her to the settee and made her lie across his knees. She was, of the two, the one who still possessed that allure of youthful romance that made him feel good coming home these days. Educated, elegant of bearing, fashionable, Ella had never failed to touch his softer part, the more vulnerable part of his soul given to a bit of the sentimental, as the young people say these days. But now, he could sense even before her unresponsive body told him so that she had something on her mind. "Tell me what the matter is Ella. You know I will listen to you."

"It's nothing," she insisted.

"Ha?" He peered into her eyes.

She did not reply. Perhaps it would be best to leave her alone; she would come around in her own time.

Ella was not without her impossible side, he knew. Naturally there were altercations now and then, stemming especially from quarrels with the first wife. Once, in fact, she had raised her dainty fingers and made to slap him. The paradox — he was left so speechless as to neither react nor say anything else — was that she was also weeping uncontrollably at the same time, and genuinely so. Both women had tussled over who should have the diamond tiara he brought back from Europe, and at the time he had been about to say it should go to Ofonne, the first, as a matter of principle, but Ella had to have it.

He gathered her to him on the sofa; she lay across his laps, still passively. At fifty-six, he often told himself he ought to be less than exactly excitable. At least so it ought to be. At times he feared that the older he got, the more he seemed to go soft in the heart. Sure, Ella was his favorite, but there were others. Would tire of these things some day — some day, he sighed. His hands went to her hips. From the slight heaving of his body, she felt what he wanted; she caught his hand and removed it. "Not now," Ella said.

Uzzi Elo was astonished; this was most unusual. Something bordering on pain threatened to cross his face but did not quite materialize. He even caught himself in a humbling change. He should have known — he admonished himself — how to handle a moody woman. Ella was downcast now; best to leave her alone. He scratched his head and shook it vigorously. He returned to the paper.

It was the sudden movement of his wife that caught his attention. She had sat bolt upright, her gaze fixed on the television. He gazed too and cried: "At last!" She said nothing, and he turned to look at her. Why was she looking so astounded? The "Bar Beach Show" was about to unfold — in his favor. What was the matter? Had they not discussed and dismissed the matter weeks ago?

"What's it now, Ella?" he queried. "Speak, woman!" A sudden anger had suddenly welled up in him.

"Did I not plead with you not to let them kill that boy?"

Uzzi Elo, were he white, might have turned red at that very moment. Instead the frown on his face turned into a grimace. Without disliking, on a spur, as was his style, the woman that was his foremost love, he certainly did not hide his anger. "Nonsense, absolute nonsense, Ella," he sputtered. "The matter with you is that you are naïve. You know as well as I do that that boy is a danger. You know well enough that if he were free, people like us would be in perpetual danger. Even imprisoning him, that is only postponing the evil day. You don't understand, woman, you don't. Life is not run on sentiment. Let me hear no more of all this pitying. People like that young man have no feelings for anyone else. Understand just that much." He paused, then added, "In any case, how could I stand in the way of justice?"

"I hear he didn't have a lawyer."

"Would that have made a difference? He was given the chance to defend himself. And he did confess. What else did he need a lawyer for? To prolong the case? His guilt was proven beyond all reasonable doubt. Now do you still blame me?"

Ella Nene Elo held her husband's arm. "No, dear. I wasn't blaming you at all. Only that I feel this public thing is not good for your image. Can't they do this in the barracks?"

Uzzi Elo laughed quietly. Disentangling himself he walked over to the bar and poured two fingers of cognac and gave one to his younger wife. "The way you talk at times, Ella!"

"Only because I am concerned for your image. You are a man of the people. How will this look?"

He shrugged, his way of conceding she had a point, but it was one nevertheless beside the main point. "That boy disgraced me, humiliated me." He could still hear those ugly, bulbous matrons sniggering at his torso, he could still recall the press jibes. His image had already taken a battering, and he had become a laughing stock. When a man reaches a certain stature, insults are never to be ignored. "You are still too young in any case," he said quietly to his wife. "Some day you will understand that I am a man whose ear no one chews to spit out."

She took the glass and drowned the contents in a gulp. With a start, she froze, crying, "Look, Uzzi, look."

And Uzzi Elo looked. The crowd was chanting and yelling. The

Black Maria had just been opened, and the condemned man was being brought down. He looked so very weak — maybe frightened. He had to be helped.

-VI-

Bar Beach, Lagos. All was set now. Close to six thousand people had turned out to witness the public spectacle. Really, he had not been too wellknown, this Aga Killam; only the papers had blown him sky-high. Not in real life was he near the notoriety of Oyenusi, the terror of Lagos, Ife, and Ibadan, who, while he lived, possessed a name that made a man shudder at its mere mention. Nor like Fineface, who had ruled the Eastern underworld. He was more like one of the several nameless small-time crooks who had met their end in this same place. But the way the story of this one had been retailed! 'Til now, for instance, no one could quite tell how many men he was said to have slaughtered — or if he indeed did kill any at all or if he had the intent to kill, in this case, having been caught with no more arms than a knife. No one, other than the police, was fully sure of anything.

The mammoth crowd stood to one side with a clear view of everything. The death row van stood in the distance facing them. Someone had scrawled on it "White Maria" — a prison clerk who had read one of V. C. Ike's novels. The condemned man had been let down and now sat on the sand, his manacled hands clasped. A strange calm had replaced the initial fear on his face. He contemplated the crowd staring at him with a philosophical air, half-listening to the priest and the pressman. A soldier pushed the latter away.

"Make de reveren' fada finish firs'," he barked. Meanwhile his fellows busily posted themselves about at strategic positions, their automatics at the ready. The armored car stood at the other side of the road, the operator's head covered with bulging earphones and goggles, visible above the war machine. To one end of the Black Maria, Captain Moh Bassey, the officer in charge of the execution, stood chatting with a lieutenant and a couple of NCOs. They also watched the men checking the rakes and the piles of empty drums behind them. Bassey had a telescope too. Occasionally he would raise it importantly and place it between his eyes. He would then scan the faces in the crowd. Next he turned to ensure that no bathers or boaters could be found on the sea within rifle-shot distance.

The reverend gentleman asked Agaranta Akandu, "Do you believe in God, my son?"

"Me, I belief in God the fada, God the son, trii in one." Aga replied, slowly looking up. His face lit up; there was mockery inscribed on it. "You hear dat? I belief in God."

The reverend, resplendent in his white cassock and black Bible bent lower still. "Are you a Christian?" he asked.

"Me, I belief in God," Aga said, "Kabisa."

"You are a Christian then?"

"I said," and there was no heat in his voice, "I trus God amighty go see all una today, dis thin' wey una dey do man pickin."

The man of God made a face and wrung his hands wondering about the follies of human nature: The youth was throwing off his last chance to salvage his sin-filled soul. But he pressed on. He had only a few more minutes. At his back hovered two mass servers with the Eucharist. He was only trying. No man knew the young man's faith. They were expecting another pastor would soon be at hand too. So if he refused the Catholic confession, then most probably he would be dispatched with Protestant felicitations instead. An imam had been contacted just in case he had turned to Islam in his years on the rampage.

The priest thus pressed on. "Are you sorry for your sins?"

"Which kin sin? Me, I no sin nothing." Aga jauntily called out to Madu and Dele hovering behind the soldiers. "You fit writ'am down make una tell de world say dis man no do nothing." At that Madu, who was with Dele in the small band of pressmen listened closely, making notes in shorthand.

The priest placed a hand on Aga's shoulder.

"I am sorry -"

The condemned man shrugged the priest off. He laughed, "For what? Sorry for what? Make una sorry for unaselfs, ojare."

The priest was understanding. "Aga, tell the Lord God thy creator. Are you sorry for what you have done?"

No answer. He repeated the question. The third time the condemned man spat out at the prelate's feet. "Wetin you dey do all dese days when dem carry me dey go from prison to court and court to prison, pillar to roof, eh? Go sorry for yaself, buo." Agaranta Akandu looked away in full contempt.

The stunned priest knew Evil when he saw it. Stepping back, the shaken man of God was quickly led away by the mass servants. He had almost lost his balance as he saw the saliva coming. He would never have imagined this. It was like the biblical Anti-Christ come to life. This one was beyond redemption.

As if sharing the reverend's sense of outrage, one of the watching privates bent down and administered a sizzling slap on Aga's face. Some in the audience would claim later that they even heard its resounding. Now the soldier drew him up. Emaciated and haggard, Agaranta Akandu — to the press Aga Killam, clearly locked worn. But he had spirit — and he reacted. For the second time he coughed and spat. The bulk of it missed a private's left eye, but particles spattered his lower cheek. He felt it sear like a spray of venom, of acid.

The enraged private swung his rifle. Now Aga showed his expertise, dropping low, in a twinkle, on his knees. The rifle butt swung overhead; the private lost his balance.

He was for coming again when the captain barked, "Enough!" He had not been looking. Dele had directed his attention on seeing the murder in the eye of the soldier, who realized almost too late that the "Bar Beach Show" was being televised. This could mean a court marshall of sorts. He glanced nervously toward the television and radio crew on their outside recording vans training their cameras and receiving transmitters in their direction.

"Ready!" he further barked.

"I've not questioned him, sir," complained Madu stepping forward. "I am from the — "

"No more questioning!" decreed the captain, turning to the firing squad. The lieutenant was already putting the twelve-man squad through their drills. Left, right! Left, right!

As two soldiers led the condemned man across to the stakes, the pressmen hurled a barrage of questions at him. It was perhaps not unexpected that he kept up the denials he had maintained, as had virtually all condemned prisoners. He said nothing else newsworthy.

Midway, something happened. A youth of about thirteen ran out of the crowd, dashing up to the prisoner, then threw himself at him weeping. Without knowing it, he had risked being cut down by a hail of fire. Who knew if he was one of Comrade Mansfrend's fools? Or anyone of the many rumored to be preparing to disrupt today's public display of moral censure? The youth was hurled away from the father he had never met; his mother had hurried with him to Bar Beach so he could see the devil who had made her pregnant and disappeared years ago. To her surprise, the boy had wanted to save him.

At exactly 5:30 p.m., with the sun going down and with the sea-waves clashing noisily, everything was set at last. A crowd of ten thousand had gathered at the beach, watching. Others were glued to television at home too, watching in the lap of civilization's most potent symbol. They saw the captain raise his baton and give the order to get ready. They saw the men clicking their guns, one step forward, fingers at the ready. They saw the swagger stick of the officer go up. To this day, some swear they saw him slam down his stick with the rasped command: "Fire!"

But everyone heard the roar of guns and saw the smoke rise and disappear. Yes, they heard the wild cheering. They saw the captain begin to motion the medical team forward as there was no need for a second hail as was customary. But few were ready for what they now saw so clearly — Aga still standing — and the executioners down? As a group of armed men came down the hills and raced to cut him free, Aga seemed to derive a new energy for the manhunt he knew would follow. Everyone heard the second wave of bullets ring out, and the four men return fire, even as the wave grew to a hail of sparks and showers, even as the terrified spectators at the Bar Beach Show took to their heels. Miraculously a good many, remembering the air raids of the civil war, hit the sands and lay still on their stomachs. Almost simultaneously — though four miles apart — both Col. Oremu and Chief Uzzi Elo shot up in their seats, astonished.

Petrified was the word.

 # A Jackpot in April

The sun came

streaming in a cheerful good-morning. Earlier than usual today, soft and caressing, it had little trouble finding the slits on the windowsills overhead. I opened my eyes, bearing witness to such regal brilliance as convinced me right away this had the makings of a day with a difference.

    I rose through the folds, yawned noisily, stretched my spare frame in four directions each for good luck, then went over to the window. Actually, picked my way would be a more apt description of what I did now as on each morning in this rented cell I call home. And fittingly enough it was sparsely furnished: a lone, weather-beaten cushion chair against the wall facing the bed and a wooden medium-sized table, groaning under the weight of the magazines and the books I usually pored through for the clerical and book-keeping exams with the Speedy Results Correspondence College Studies in far-away London. The chair and the table dominated the room. There was also the low stool in the center, atop which rested my most impressive glass jug. And there was a carpet too, a red, once-pretty affair that gave a glowing hue to the sun-kissed room. Deliberately hidden by the door stood a pile of boxes and a chest of drawers, cupboard, as we called it, an aged wooden cabinet that contained my pots and pans. The aroma of the soup I made last night hung in the air, turning my stomach.

I flung open the window and looked out at the world. Again the sun! How it came in sudden explosion, bearing with it a cool breeze, blinding for a moment, exhilarating the rest of the time. I gazed up across roof-tops to see if indeed it had correctly risen in the East so it might later set in the West.

"Good morning, sir!" chorused a group of boys giving the landlord's Peugeot wagon a wash.

"Morning, boys!" I waved at them. I could see them very well because my room gave on to the street. The oldest was fourteen; the youngest, eight. Then I added the customary admonition. "Don't be late to school. Remember, school is progress!"

"They won't," boomed a familiar voice. It belonged to their father. The boys — five of them — were his offspring. His had been an unusually late marriage, and this was their collective morning chore. We called him Chief Haw-Haw on account of his large sense of humor.

"My chief, my salutations!" Leaning out of the window so he could see me well enough, I bowed slightly and gave a military-style salute, for we had all over the years become accustomed to angry soldiers, rulers whose most enduring contribution to everyday speech was the "with immediate effect" ending of their many broadcasts. He had stepped onto the veranda, his fingers also up in salute, his legs doing the martial steps he had learnt as a foot soldier in the

British West African Frontier Force (WAFF) decades ago. I'd heard it said he had trained under some of the surviving British officers who at the turn of the century had taken part in the storming of the ramparts of the Sokoto Caliphate, which meant he should be over seventy. He had been cashiered by the Nigerian Army for having fought on the losing Biafran side, but his large old soldier's sense of humor never faded. On those mornings when the spirit took us, we would re-enact the generational gap for all to see: Our salute postures were as different as our ages! I had learnt mine imitating the lean and sullen soldiers of the civil war.

"Now look at this, Nkele, look!" I watched him strut the potent steps of war. About turn. Forward, march. Eyes front. Salute. Right turn, left turn. Left, right, left, right. Forward, slow march. Ha-a-halt! Cheering came forth from the neighbors and from his sons. At this moment everyone was out to savor the sun, and Chief Haw-Haw's pumpkin-size midstomach was only too well-known along our street's row of houses built to standard, like match boxes.

"Can you do that, Soft One?" he taunted, turning towards me. But I made no reply. Which was unusual. He noticed at once. He followed my eyes, riveted as they were on the young woman in the white flowered dress gracefully entering the taxi that had stopped in front of the next house. Enene, that was her name. I held my breath watching as she gave the driver instructions, peered as the exhaust fumes defied even the sun to cast a shadow over half the place, gazed as the car drove off with her. It was like this any morning I was fortunate to see her go off to work. I would just stand and gape. I turned to the landlord. "In your time, ever saw anything like her, mazi?"

But the old man merely laughed. "In my time, Soft One, we never watched from a distance."

Curious, I leant farther out of the window and asked: "So how was it in those days?"

He undid and redid his folds of wrapper, shook his head with its shock of grey hair and smacked his lips mischievously. "Simple," he said. "Very simple, Nkele, we just walked up to them. They don't bite. How do you think I forgot to marry while my age-mates became grandfathers?" Then, chuckling loudly, he turned to keep his watch on the boys.

I thought there was something to what he said, but that was only the saying of it. Two young men across the street who kept a provisions store waved at me. I waved back, and we shouted good morning at each other. On more than a single occasion, they had said they would give anything to be like me, to work in a government office, dress up each morning, shoes polished, a suit and tie each morning, walk off each day with a rolled umbrella, rain or shine. At times I had in turn wished they knew what really was on my mind; but as a rule I never practiced being a shriveller of dreams. At times they could be good even for sheer sanity.

I stood by the window a while longer, watching the early morning stream of men and women emerging from their cells. Bigger and better cells maybe. Like ants in their wisdom, everyone and everything on the move in response to a certain compulsion, part of our common lot. Then I turned to get ready for work, without much pleasure. As usual, however, two things preoccupied me. Would I get a place in the university admissions this year? Where would the money come from if I did? For years now I had been staking at the pools, betting on the Leeds and London teams, once in a while favoring the Dundee United, but hoping for the big one any of these days. For the pittance I had grasped, the rest of the pay check had gone down the whirlpool. What funny rhythm: For every one place in the university, thirty people scrambled; for every six Naira earned, two dripped down the pools drainage. Yet like all learned habits, a certain compulsion resists the logic of giving up a game with more cons than pros. Then I got ready and left for my clerk's Grade 3 job at the Ministry.

But the start of the narrative I now relate should be placed hours later that same day. The rapping on the door of my room had come at about four-fifteen. I had left the office early, at three rather than four, a little sick, tired out, for it had been a dull, moody day. The knocks came on again. They came in pairs, rasping. Who could that be? Certainly not Benji Ibara. Only he would have gone on rapping at my door this way — we had been friends since we were boys. But he wouldn't be back in town until tomorrow, I thought, having gone off to Aba to sit for his Secondary School Teacher's Qualifying Examination. For some strange reason now I experienced a certain numbness, unwilling to go to the door or peer out of the window. Once again the knocks. Something uncanny about them, I could have sworn. Slowly I edged towards it, taking courage from the sunny rays still screaming in. My hands were already at the doorknob when I heard the familiar swear words; with a laugh I swung open the door to reveal that it was indeed the ubiquitous pools betting agent.

"Igu!" I cried. But there was hardly any smile on his wound-scarred face, the result of bottle fights at bar room brawls one full generation earlier. His otherwise unkempt hair as usual was drawn backward, his danshiki shirt over his worn trousers shabby, his sandals threadbare at the edges. His head shook vigorously, signifying some issue he disapproved of. "I always told you, young man," he intoned, still motioning for the most part with his head, "at least I tried, young man, to tell you and the others, women and serious business never go together."

Now, that was all he said — as yet. But the impact of those few words was electrifying. The question that had formed in my mouth, that could have long left my lips, simply got stuck. For women, aside from higher education and a run of ill luck at football pools betting, remain my one most outstanding failure. They invariably would gaze down my small height or through my admittedly not too bulging pockets, and declare me a write-off. "Women?" I queried, my voice sinking much lower than my heart had managed moments ago. "Women? What women?"

"Yes, women," declared Igu Eweka most emphatically, spitting the word, "women and serious business. You might well have missed me."

"But there is no lady here," I informed him.

His head stopped shaking in its intense disapproval. With one deft move, much as a puff-adder on the loose might have done, he stuck his head right over mine — he towers above me — and through the curtain. Precisely at this moment, I hit on the explanation for this. It all had to do with the puzzle of God's fairer sex, yes. His young wife had only three months ago made off with his entire fortune, raw cash that ran into the five figures, it was said. She had last been heard of in faraway Lagos, where she could be counted upon to make friends powerful enough to scare off her husband's own truly frightful strong-arms here in Umuahia. She had been the only person he ever trusted, so the word went; ever since her disappearance, he was said not to be sure even of his own shadow. But we younger men who crammed his place on weekends could tell these were mere beer-table tales spread by his enemies.

I still remember the first time we met. That had been three years back. I had come to Umuahia to work, after secondary school in Enugu. Benji Ibara and I had been to school together, separated for a year, only to meet again at Umuahia as young civil servants. He had arrived here before me and knew the lay of the land fairly well. He it was who had first taken me to Igu's place. It was a large house with two wings. One served as the pools office where we staked the odds and made faces each time nothing came of it. The other was the beer parlor run by his wife from a second or third marriage — we were never quite sure which; here we went to drink and sing when we won a few naira, here the game's addicts would sit pondering over their bottles, brooding being more like it. Now and then there would be a fight. On one such occasion Igu Eweka had had to intervene, physically hurling the rascals through the window. That had been my first night there. While Benji had laughed away, I had watched in total disbelief. That was how Igu had first noticed me.

"You don't belong here," he said, pointing at me. What could I say? There was something to that. Months later, after we had become better acquainted, he told me he thought I was a police spy. Today, we had become more like old friends of sorts

Now his wife was gone, and the beer parlor was closed. But the other section still thrived, though some old hands believe part of the vigor of the place had gone with the woman.

With a sigh he withdrew his head from the curtains like some wizened tortoise backing into its shell. I wondered about the latest bets. Winning was out of the question for me — only pittances might come, as usual. "What makes you remember me today, Igu Eweka? I never saw the toad out in broad daylight."

For answer he steeped into my cell, with the words "bottle of whisky" trailing his steps; he had this drawl-mumbling way of speaking that not a few times had the effect of making you lose the meat of what he said, even as you grasped the flavor.

Bottle of whisky? The moment I finally made out the words, their meaning came rushing at me, cascading my entire being, much as the sun and the cool air of fading dawn enveloped one in the morning.

The results were out. Had I hit a bull's eye? The Jackpot? Certainly — could it be anything else? I queried him anxiously. "Is it the jackpot?" Clearly that was a needless concern, for surely it was.

He stroked his greying beard, adjusting himself on the lone cushion chair into which he had lowered his sizeable bulk. Oh, I should mention this — that consistent with nature's studied calculation to make him different, Igu Eweka remains to this day the only man I ever saw whose frame was as round and bulging as his head was oblong and receding. The beard, this time of his own creation, running down in two divisions, quite completed the picture of one who was at once with us and not of us. His cronies swore every other day the man was a guru of sorts whose forecast, when he deigned to make one, never failed to strike home, as it is said. Trouble being that he hardly ever would forecast. Once, however — the Dundee United vs. the Liverpool Lions, I think it was — at the Grand Raffle, he had cast an idea in my direction. Though it came to nothing, it had made sense at first. Yes, fearful as his visage purports, Igu, as I'd said before, was our man any day.

"How much?" I could, naturally, hardly contain myself, though in fairness I did try to still the wild flip-flops of my heart by placing a hand over my chest.

Igu Eweka picked his words slowly. "Enough to make you never forget this game, my boy."

That sounded double-layered, but this was beside the point now. Igu had always been strange in his ways. With him you expect nothing to come tumbling out neat and straight. Like the snake in the bag, he would respond only to the charmer's continued fluting. That was a fact we had learnt at his place weekend after weekend as we had sat and put the marks on the pool sheets, the sound of music and the smell of wine heavy in the air.

I shook his hands again, the spirit filled and overflowing. Who could have foreseen such a turn only this morning? This single thought pervaded me, coming and going on my mind, like the neon signs on the cigarette advertising boards. Only this time, the grand buildings of the University at Nsukka kept winking at me, affectionately for the first time, its gates swinging open, its bright flowered drive in most sunny welcome.

The pools agent said, reading my mind, "Perseverance, my boy, that's what we say." For the first time he raised his face, that virtual minefield of experience sublime and savory, and gazed at me and said: "Nkele, never forget the old saying — 'every dark cloud has its silver lining.' To play the game is a way to say you dare to dream of better things in this life!" And so saying he burst into a low, deep-throated laughter. But I was only aware, not hearing. I could see before me the unfolding of the narrow path running into the great broad road to the future. True enough my approach to it had been a test of the will to call the bluff of destiny, to rise beyond an endless pull to despondency. From desk to desk at the offices, I had both worried and dreamt of universities here and across the seven cities and out there across the seven oceans. Money it was that had long strapped me to those bare chairs wearing off my backsides, trading files and gossips with three plump, ever chattering girls for whom life meant no more than literally tackling and capturing some well-off fool. They had not surprisingly missed the intellectual in me: every one of them, I even remember, had gazed through my bones and, again permit my saying so a second time, seen through my lean pockets. Now, at last! My turn to stand tall, despite my inconsequential height!

Igu Eweka withdrew his hands from his pockets, automatically flying them to his grey beard. His eye sparkled and his lips quivered. "Your father should have taught you better manners," he began, speaking faster than normal. But I had a swift interjection:

"My father died ten years ago."

"Then your mother— "

"Well," I began, "I never had any."

The expression that came over his face was not one of astonishment; it was plain annoyance. He gazed at me for a long while. Then he spoke. "How old are you, Nkele?"

"Enough to find my way about, Mazi Eweka," I laughed and went over to draw the window curtain to keep away part of the late sun streaming in. But I relented. "If you must know, I was born twenty-five harmattans ago." I meant the cold but sunny harmattan seasons of early January each year; bearing down the forested south from the northern savannah regions of this country, it possessed a particularly ominous ring of a world about to end, as lips would chap, noses run and skins become parched.

Igu's mask did not change. I began to laugh again. Actually, I liked these half-comic moods of his, this misplaced paternalism. But he was taking his time. I longed to know the details of this windfall, though something cautioned against rushing the old man. Let him come to the point his own way, I concluded. He cut into my laughter. "Those are enough years to have given you something more —" He checked himself. "What do you mean you never had any mother?"

"You want to know ?" I asked. He nodded.

My voice was dry and crackled as I related how this unusual

problem had arisen. My father, who had lived all his forty years in the north, had been unable to settle in any profession with a name nor, for any length of time, with any female. One, though, had borne him a child, an event he had regarded as the only worthwhile occurrence in an otherwise pedestrian, peripatetic existence. Accordingly, rather than lose me to a woman who like the rest was about to desert him, he had instead chosen to turn the tables and himself be the deserter, with me in tow of course. In the fifties when all this was taking place, the vast territory of Her Brittanic Majesty's Colony of Nigeria, especially its northern vastness, was such that anyone accustomed to his lifestyle could literally vanish into thin air. He had first kept me with an aunt for three years, then brought me back to his household from where I left to attend one of those cheap community secondary schools, whose main asset was its dormitories. And despite my asking over the years, he never made mention of my mother, the woman who had given me birth, no clue whatsoever beyond hinting that someday when I could understand, we would talk more about it. But that day was never to be, for during a trip up north by rail, he had been pushed off into the river following a brawl. His body was never found. Indeed stories were eventually to reach me that a woman — a woman that had seemed to know him in the past — had been behind the accident. But that had only been a rumor. No one — neither the police nor the train officials nor those who peddled the stories — had been able either to identify the woman, nor effect any arrests.

"A sad story indeed," said Igu Eweka as I brought my tale to an end. "But make no mistakes young man, don't think you are the only one with a story that could make a man walk away from his afternoon meal." His hands moved, predictably flying to his bearded jaw, drawing on the double-jutting mass of hair. A story was certainly in the making. "I, too, upon whom you gaze now," he began, "I am myself a story wrapped complete and whole in mysteries you would never understand. To look at me just once is to guess the truth. Yes, I had neither mother nor father at all." He paused, his hands back at the jaw. He always employed both hands. What was he really saying?

"What does that mean, Igu?"

"It means this, I only heard that someone or maybe two people, it doesn't really matter, actually gave birth to me. But since they both died on the same day soon after I was born, I cannot say I had any parents." His sunken eyes glared at me, making me shift my gaze.

"But someone must have looked after you," I said, forgetting to ask the most obvious question of how both could have died the same day.

"I can tell you I remember many people who tried. They were my people of course. But I can also tell you, from the first moment this world's dirty air rushed into me, making me shed my first tear in life, young man, I have been on my own." He raised a hand. "I don't want to go on with this grandmother's tale. My whisky, quick!"

But he had aroused my interest. There was something sad and weary in his voice. I had heard he once was a teacher in the township elementary school. "But who saw you through the teacher training college?"

He thumped his chest. "Who else?"

"You found the money?" I knew how it had been for anyone whose background in the thirties was that lamentable even among a people so impoverished, orphaned, and with no strong backers. Those who ever rose from the dust had done so mostly through trading, not schooling. If, however, it came about that they had managed through the village school for three years when added up, it was next to impossible to have gone beyond the spell-thy-name, count-thy-toes, count-thy-fingers stage. "How did you find the money?" I asked again, genuinely curious.

For answer, Igu Eweka burst into laughter. "I can see only very clearly there are two things on your mind," he said, his tone changing, his laughter ending in mid-air like bad music that ceases midstream. Upon some instinct, I stepped away from him, moving over to the little bed, conveniently spaced as far as the cell — my room, that is — could allow. Igu Eweka, apparently took no notice of the apprehension he had created. Yet from what I knew, there was enough mercury in him to turn his mood around without warning.

"The two things in your mind," he went on, "are that either I tricked those missionaries into believing I cared for their Three-in-One, or else I had spent my time stealing supplies for the soldiers bound for the Cameroons and quartered in my village for weeks, eh?"

The question was hurled rather than directed at me; it struck me, making me respond involuntarily: "I don't really know." Now this was an answer I ordinarily wouldn't have given in any such situation, since I knew, indeed I had heard it said, you don't ever have to know a story to the full, something of everything is enough. Which was why the girls in the office thought I had too much of a book-loving disposition than was good for a struggling clerk. Indeed, my superior had chosen, I suspect, partly on account of my never being humble enough to say I had doubts about anything, not to recommend me for promotion, though just a mere shift to one more desk. But I made a quick recovery. "So then," I pressed him once more, "tell me how you made it."

"I am surprised," he began, "that you continue to underrate

the magic of football pools betting — "

"You mean the money came from —"

He gave a series of grunts that just couldn't pass for laughter. "Where else?" He then swung his head to an angle so his eyes pierced mine — actually searing the balls of my eyes — like a practiced hypnotist. "I don't have the whole day, young man, that's the first thing. Second, I am dying of thirst. Where's the whisky! I thought you had manners from your family. Well, I have heard your story. So what? Go get the whisky." Something in his manner struck me as odd; how does one deal with the likes of Igu Eweka?

"But you have told me nothing," I protested. True enough the harbinger of good tidings deserves rewards — but not until his burden is laid.

His eyes sank back into their hollow, snapping; his head fell back on the cushion. That was his answer. At that precise moment the sun beams dulled as the first evening shadow crossed the face of the brilliant firmament, that star which, it is said, holds the earth at the mercy of its rays. It only had to cease to shine, and we all are as good as bound for suffocation — at least so the biology mistress had bade us, then of the senior class, never forget. That had been years ago, and we had just been on the verge of being unleashed upon a world not exactly ready for us.

Without looking at the sun, I went out to find Igu Eweka his whisky. The noise of his snoring dogged my steps as I edged outside; he was apparently not faking sleep. That did not change the fact of my lean pockets — nor that I would have to buy on credit.

An hour after he had gone, I set out for Igu's place as arranged. With the two hands dug into the pockets of my tight-fitting trousers, I stood before the half-closed door to Enene's room. It was in the very next building. I knew like everyone else, she was back for the day, preparing her evening meal perhaps. Three raps on the wooden panel brought her to the door. You should have seen the look on her face: The frown made a classic contrast to my full-lip smile.

"Enene!" I hailed the pretty lady, my face necessarily tilted in an upward angle. Though my friend Benji Ibara had sworn she was no more than merely of average height and passable beauty, she had never appeared less than being up there, a giant of sorts among the truly fair. Round-faced, soft, and elegant. Her sort, sir, I would never fail to hanker after. People had said this has something to do with my being short, but that's not true.

"Oh, it's you, Nkele. What do you want?" she asked, gazing quickly around, or so it seemed to me. I had never asked her — indeed never sought to know — if she had anyone close to her heart. The way she looked at the other rooms in this rectangular courtyard suddenly brought the matter to the fore. Still — this was not the time to say a word on it.

"Haven't you heard?" I began lamely, pulling my already close-fitting clothes about me in a manner I have long suspected made no little impression on women. The news of the jackpot had spread in the building where I lived. I had met Chief Haw-Haw at the wine shop — indeed he had paid for the whisky. He said they would all be waiting for me to declare "surplus" for everyone tonight — and receive accolades fitting enough for my newly risen station in life. It was then I had made up my mind to stop by Enene's before hurrying off to Igu's.

"Heard what?" There was no trace in her tone of any change, any desire to know; I sensed that she would be glad if I turned on my heels, lowered my standard, like any dog twisting its tail between thighs, and fled! But I would do nothing of the sort. I had longed for this day — when I could ask her to visit or go shopping on my account, or perhaps come see a film show with me.

"What would you say if I told you — and mark you, you're the first I am telling — that I just won thousands in my name at this moment?" I watched her closely; I was still tense. What would she say? As it was, the expression on her face underwent no change. In that fleeting moment it was all I could do to prevent my heart bursting as my breath got stuck, my palms beginning to get wet. But it was only a moment, a fleeting moment. I began to feel silly; this was no way to get to anyone's good side, much less, I suspected, the likes of Enene. But how else? As everyone knew, you either have to be prepared with bulging pockets — or else be possessed of the sweetest tongue.

The girl took a deep breath, then said, "That would be good for you." That was all she said. Why I had expected her to say more than this, I cannot now spell out, save that I had been under the spell of my own hopes and fears. For a full long minute, we stood facing each other, the sun playing off our eyeballs. I could see its roundness in the black of each eye, unconsciously noticing how it revolved each time she rolled them above and across my head. Everyone was taller than I. Igu Eweka, Benji Ibara, Enene, my father, maybe my mother.

"Can I come in?" I finally asked.

"You want to?" she asked, opening the panel grating that guarded against the slanting rain of these parts from coming in. "I thought you didn't want to." There was nothing in her expression to indicate she would be willing to spend two moments thinking about me. But as I stepped in, my back awash with the last rays of the sun, nothing would have convinced me I hadn't come half-way at least.

For you see, my longing for Enene has always been from a distance. Oh, to be sure I had come near enough once or twice to give her a wink and endeavor to say something without ever saying much. She was one of those people possessed of that charm, that far-off bearing that never failed to stir the desire of all who recognized and admired beauty for what it was — a charm that inspires the courage to take the first step — the spirit that takes its cue from the film shows we've grown to adore. Each time however, the acid-tongued Benji would never fail to point out that when it came to spirit and courage, I lacked the one no less than I possessed the other as far as Enene was concerned. Else why all the distant infatuation? They had laughed at me, made table-top music linking my name with hers; that had been a month and a half ago at Igu's. But as far as I was concerned, everything they had to say became meaningless once Benji and Tony and Ewere and Hassan had insinuated that since beauty was in the eye of the beholder, it was pointless explaining to me just how this female paragon of mine was nothing really unusual. But I needed no lesson from anyone about envy. They would be first to rise to their feet if they thought they stood a chance. I knew that. Or more to the point, if they had the spirit.

"Sit down," said Enene. She had no idea what had flashed through my mind in those fifty seconds as I entered her cell: she, too, was a working girl as the newspapers now call female office clerks. She would never know how much she has been discussed at her back, never know how much I had followed her steps in the deep recesses of my heart in the morning, as she went to work and each weekend as she went to market. How would she have known that I had once grown sick with longing? "Do you want something to drink?" she asked.

"Anything," I said, answering two questions, one unasked yet, at the same time.

She had one of those refrigerators now flooding everywhere from Japan or Taiwan. And there was Coca Cola in it too, which was more important: I adored the carbonated mixture. She fetched one and retrieved a glass cup and went out to wash it at the common running water tap at the end of the enclosed courtyard; I could hear her humming the hit song of the season, a song that had come all the way from the United States, which the local slang-slinging disc jockeys had continued to blare on radios across the nation. This one was even said to have held the first spot on the Radio Nigeria Enugu FM station's "Top Ten" charts for two months running. "Live and Let Love Be Love," it was called. Which by the way was to say that a girl who could hum a popular rock 'n roll tune was in touch with things.

And it all reflected in her taste, shone like the stars all over her room. While my place was no more than a cell of claustrophobia, the very contrast was true in hers — a feeling of space was what one got here: a table by the window, an array of bottles and of perfumes and toiletteries, a pile of novels — I spotted Agatha Christie and Flora Nwapa and Mabel Segun — a large mirror, a hair coiffure gadget, large and little combs and other odds and ends you find on women's tables, I guess. The light pink-flowered curtain hanging on the window over the table gave a certain serenity to a framed photograph of her resting at the center itself. I had no second thoughts about how wonderful, how charming she looked.

Nor was the rest of the room any less enchanting. Three cane chairs, light brown in color, ringed a low, round wooden table atop which stood a plastic red-and-green-bottled hibiscus. A Bible, the St. James version, silver embossed, stood next to the flowers. Was she religious? With a pang I recalled I had not been to church in months. And the way she made her bed and arranged her dresses and hid her boxes underneath the bed, how her pots and pans had sparkled when she had opened the wooden cupboard where she kept such utensils! They were a far cry from my disorder. And the floor beyond the grey and white carpet sparkled, evidence of good scrubbing.

I had not noticed the second framed photograph in good time, but then I did. There she was, perhaps a little younger, laughing, held aloft by someone — yes, a man, not old at all! My heart did one of those flip-flops but this time far more in a sinking direction.

"That's my father."

I swung around; she had just walked in. "Your father?" My voice shook a little; no one likes getting caught, I guess, trying to fit things together.

"Yes. Don't you like him? You look — "

"Oh, no! Yes, yes — of course —" I swiftly tendered a few more protestations of my reverence — a factor that had not exactly occurred to me when I had been observing the picture; its intimacy was the one thing that held me as I wondered who he could have been. "Where is he?"

"At the University of Nigeria," she said.

"He's not a student, is he?"

She laughed rather gaily. "Oh, no. He's a professor."

I couldn't have heard right. "What did you say?"

She had just finished placing the cup and the coke and gone over to one of the cane chairs, the one nearest the table. "About my father? He teaches at Nsukka." Her voice was casual.

"Really? Interesting." I muttered a few more incomprehensible words about how nice it would have been living in such an ivory tower, meanwhile reaching for my drink, pouring the dark brown sugary liquid into the cup, hiding my astonishment. So what is she doing here? Ought to be abroad studying somewhere like all the rest, eh? Should have long suspected she was born with some sort of spoon right in between her teeth; I had initially put her down for a firm good silver, the sort they mine over the backs of sad people down in South Africa. Now it may well be gold — or diamond — or platinum, depending.

She broke the silence. "You work at the Ministry of Internal Affairs?"

"Yes. And you work at Health?" We knew this much about each other.

"Yes. Do you like your office?"

I made a face. "You won't believe me if I told you."

She laughed. "Tell me," she requested. "I want to hear."

I took a sip. "I don't like recalling the office."

"Then why don't you leave the place?" There was concern in her voice.

"Because I have no choice." Enene had no answer to that, so I asked the obvious question. "You must love your work."

She opened a bottle of Coca Cola she had and took a sip; it was good watching her. She appeared relaxed, my company perhaps not as burdensome as I had feared. Her face radiant, she finally made a reply. "Of course," she said, "I like my work. Very much. Perhaps that's why I won't believe you don't."

"You mean you like shifting files, answering calls, that sort of thing?"

"Why not? You work and you chat with everyone."

"I hate gossips," I said, trying to sound right; she said life would be too boring without lively talk. Still I did remember the girls at the office and their endless chattering. But it was different, Oh, yes, listening to Enene talk, I never dreamt she would be so friendly.

Yet she said nothing about the jackpot, not even a condescending reference. From the first it had not seemed to interest her. But there was no doubting as we conversed that she was becoming more curious; I refuse to say "interested," lest that reads askance. Yes, she did ply me with questions. How old are you? Where were you born? Your parents? What have you been doing all these years? Do you do any sports? But can you stand on your head and dance round and round like the Igodo masquerade? Oh, no? Why not?

And it was no one-way affair. She did tell about herself too. She had been born in London where her parents had been at school and had met as students. The family had returned shortly before the civil war erupted and had been rendered homeless during the fighting itself like ten million others. She still had vivid memories of the entire family, by the widest stretch of association, the entire clan as it were, trailing behind her father, who still had useful contacts here and there, refugees marching from one Red Cross center to the next, a daily struggle not to wither away like the countless many drooping lifeless by the wayside.

She had attended one of those closely-fenced Queen's Colleges and was now out in the work force so as to feel the real world. Her father, a rather practical man, had suggested it might not be such a bad idea for her to work awhile before thinking of the university. Of course I said that was a wonderful idea.

How had she found the town so far?

"Dull," she said laughing, "except for the office."

But her parents drove down each month to see how she was doing. An uncle lived a street or two away in any case; she usually spent Sundays with him and his family.

Yet she said not a word on the fact that I was this day several thousands better than I had been when I woke this morning.

"Do you know I watch you each morning as you leave for work?" I asked her.

Again she laughed; she had this constant laughing side I never dreamt was there. "You think I don't know? I see through the rear window of the taxi cabs!"

I felt ashamed a little; one doesn't like getting caught trying to....

Then she shot forth another question: "But why do you look at me that way each morning?" Her eyes pressed on mine from that distance. Her face was all intensity, yet there was no hostility implied or felt, but there was no concealing her curiosity.

I had no answer — no direct answer, I mean. I just gazed back at her, smiling wider than I had done at her doorway thirty minutes earlier, hoping she would understand.

We talked of music — Fela was still the big news of the age, as was JB, the King of Soul. We chatted about how we so loved good films. Had she seen *The Guns of Iva Valley* yet? It was one of the few good Nigerian-made films. Then with a quick glance at my watch, I announced I had to leave at once to go pick up my win.

She looked at me, began to say something, then changed her mind. At the door she asked where Igu's office was; I told her.

"You are welcome to stake with us," I said. "Can I come by again?"

She laughed and shrugged; I thought she also nodded. I left unsure of how to fit things now; she had avoided asking anything more.

****

Igu Eweka's place was at the other end of the next street. One could make it in ten minutes at dawn when men and matter, animals and — yes — those countless creaking lorries, were all still half-asleep. But now I picked my way along the dusty streets fully aware that any of those drivers could lose control or, as often as not, drive me off the good parts. There are indeed at all times and in all places struggles of sorts, I would imagine.

"Orange?" A pretty but sad-faced teenage schoolgirl still in her uniform held out a bunch of the fruits; she carried scores of them, delicately balanced on her head, some green, some peeled to their white and yellow flesh. A tarpaulin cover offered protection from the sun.

I shook my head and passed on along. Neither oranges nor orange girls could bother me now. Two things fully took up all available space in my mind — don't imagine these things can't be estimated! The truth was that Enene took virtually all of it, but my immediate mission was beginning to make spirited demands.

"Buy groun'nuts!" Yet another youngster, this time a boy. Good children, I thought momentarily, helping raise their school fees. But I would buy no nanas nor nuts and no regrets either: this was not the time. A Peugeot wagon careening down the street literally hurled me onto the pavement of one of the houses as it rolled past. A group of bulky women buying danshiki dresses for their children from a Hausa trader took no notice of me. But one of the little ones had laughed at my not too dignified retreat from the street; when you brave the heat to put on a striped tie and dark suit, everyone believes came home with you from abroad, you don't let anything rattle you. I had broken an etiquette there. The sharp blaring of more car horns promptly sent me back to the pavement; a rare police patrol car swung the corner, heading after the first car. Must either be some criminal in flight or a taxi driver unwilling to come to terms, who had perhaps not dipped deep enough into his day's takes...

The sun dimmed a third time.

Igu had asked me to come over as soon as I could. He had

refused, indeed as he swore, never to let me know anything until I had brought his whisky. And I hadn't had enough to pay. But as it was, this was one of those lucky days. I had gone over to the shop across the street next to my house. The two young men who waved at me each morning and dreamt of being civil servants and wearing ties like me had been very appreciative but could do no more than that. The master had only days before issued a proclamation: no more credits! My stomach did then turn — but not for the sake of bananas, which often had that effect on me; these ones didn't seem ripe yellow enough in any case. The point was that people like me simply lived off monthly credits from shops like this — what with taxi fares and cinema tickets and good beer amidst good songs, what with staking at the pools and dreaming of universities all over the place!

But my landlord had saved me, as I mentioned earlier. Chief Haw-Haw had stepped in precisely at that moment to buy a fresh tin of Erimo imported tobacco to fill his pipe; one of his sons rounding off his law studies at the Lincoln's Inn in London had sent it to mark the old man's recovery from a long bout of malaria. He had sensed that great things were in the air; he was right of course. And in being right about it and not wishing for the great thing to escape, he had ended up paying for a bottle of good imported whisky. He and the rest — his boys and my fellow tenants — would be in wait for me to return. But I have said this before.

"Daily Times! New Nigerian!" The newsboy with a blowhorn caught my attention; but I did not care for his paper. Who wanted to hear about the latest government scandal?

Something had been nagging at me for a while now. What would be the best thing to do with the fortune? No, I don't mean where to hide the haul. One thing for sure, tomorrow morning, I would have to demand to see the bank manager first thing. How his beefy cheek would smile up at me. Once I had gone to borrow a little from the bank to pay up my Speedy Results fees; the front office clerk had first browsed through me from head to toe — believe me when I say I felt this — before telling me the manager was "too busy." The logic of money would now demand that he fling the little gate to the manager's section open as soon as I came in sight. I began to chuckle.

"Look where you go!" barked a ragged man; I had no doubt he had had more marijuana sniffs than was good for him. Or maybe he was drunk on wine. "Your father, you mother!" he cursed. My ire rose like fire on fuel. One's parents remain sacred, even if you hardly knew one and the other was dead. He still stood there looking at me. But he first bumped into me.

"He's sick in the head," a middle-aged woman who lived in one of the houses cried out at me from her doorway.

"Dalu, thank you," I said and hurried on; in fact she needn't have worried I was going to challenge the craggy fellow, no matter what honor demanded. His madness had shone in his eyes, leaping out like tongues of flame. And I was not yet blind.

Igu Eweka's place was no more than a few more minutes. The Uzuakoli road, the major artery dissecting this side of town, led to the Ogwumabiri marketplace and beyond. From it one makes his way on the day-long bus ride to the heart of the land, to the capital city, where Igu's wife had run off with his stored wealth. What was I going to do with this windfall? Go into business? I pondered the idea. Moments later, I confessed to myself, how tempting! Just a question of seeing the right people and doing the right things, and I would be in the import-export business. Was I still young enough to benefit from the University? In any case, why bother about a university degree when the money was finally on my lap? Now, now, why give ears to those who hold those lofty ideas about pursuing higher education as an end in itself? Those people who run our lives for salaries in the six figures, as the Americans would say, and on the basis of the academic degrees worn like amulets, they would be the ones to tell you the baccalaureate was investment enough. A battle raged in my soul between my intellectual disposition and the logic of money-making in a harsh country where to be poor was to be without a name.

There were no more vehicles coming. I dashed across the road and disappeared into yet one more side street. In moments such as the present, you did not wish to expose yourself lest some envious devil was loose on the trail out for you.

I passed the two-story mansion of the great lawyer, barrister Samuel F. F. Ekwekwe, his last name fitting his penchant for all manner of tactics, written and unwritten, that stopped at nothing to swing a case; a notable brothel, too, stood next to his chambers, its scores of cigar-smoking sweet women, as we say, impatiently awaiting the descent of darkness. Then the men would begin to sneak in; then they would all begin to get drunk; then eyes would begin to turn to the great barrister and the court cases, the murder cases, the maiming cases, the rape, yes, the rape cases.

I turned the corner, crossed the rail tracks, and stepped into the other half of town, onto the other major tarred highway that led on all the way to the commercial city of Aba and the oil fields and wharves of Port Harcourt. Still separated by the roadway, I stood before Igu Eweka's place, Igu's Football Stakes House. Indeed I could spot the sign of his business from this distance; in times like this your eyes acquire powers of penetration you never knew were there. I gazed across the lorries and the cars, not really noticing them; my eyes glazed past the sun-swept walls of the storied houses; having to look at people was a chore. Just a single thought filled my lungs, swelled my heart. How much? How large was that jackpot? I have heard it said that people have been known to go whirli-gigging crazy when mother luck throws her gauntlet! Oh, but it's not so fanciful.

Every other step brought me nearer; it was like stepping on air-springs, those wonder gadgets of childhood tell-tales. I thought of Enene; she had not appeared astonished or excited, thanks to her golden spoon. But — did she really mean I could come again, perhaps have dinner with her?

"Nkele!" There was no mistaking Benji Ibara's voice. The dark blue Volkswagen pulled up, panting beside me; other cars immediately massed up behind him.

"Benji, you!" I leaned over to the window; a girl sat to his right, a fresh face as usual. "You are early. When did you come back?"

"Just coming," he said, his mustachioed upper lip making funny patterns as he spoke like one sputtering. He was my best friend, and I was dying to let him know. But I had barely opened up when he cried out: "I'll meet you in ten minutes!" He winked at the girl. I understood. There was even greater danger in the form of the honking, cursing drivers at his tail; two had in fact stepped out and were bearing down toward us when Benji let go of the clutch and stole the thunder on them. Benji it was who had first taken me to Igu Eweka's, first taught me how to stake. Like me, he worked for the government, like me he spent every waking hour dreaming of the university, of the money to stake his claim to life. We drank beer together, and we eyed the same girls; but if it came about, he would surely faint at my Enene upset, above all else.

I finally stood at the entrance to Igu Eweka's pools office, like a triumphant supplicant summoned by the gods to the shrine; at the holy place you are expectant, and you are fearful. The two are never far apart. But now hope was on the ascendant.

There must have been close to twenty men there, half of them studying the long notice boards; the results, I thought. The rest either stood inside or sat on the benches outside, faces drawn, arms folded across their chests; the losers no doubt. Inside, two men argued in loud voices, even as they danced to the throbs of a high-life music from Igu's "record changer": minor winners, these, losers of a different sort. They held glasses of whisky, their eyes red, their lips hanging. The sun made a sudden return, splashing everything. Still on my airy springs, I stepped into the place, ready to lift my prize. I had staked and lost money here three years running. Now!

Nothing happened. The agent was there alright. Igu Eweka had seen me where I stood, two hands dug deep in two pockets. Yet he made no move to welcome me, nor cry for order among the babbling lot, to announce in a loud voice: "Quiet everyone! The jackpot chief himself is here at last!" I had even warned myself there should be no surprise, no resistance when he bids three of his best strong-arms lift me off my feet, whirl me about the place, in celebration; no surprise when those present demanded a feast of beer, a wine-pot for any man that had the goodwill to ask. It was not every other day that windfalls arrive.

Still nothing happened. Something turned in my stomach, a stiff knock all of a sudden. What it was I have never known to this day. But my eyes were turning red. What was up? I had seen jackpot winners crowned on this same floor enough times. Maybe my youth, maybe my person? I craned my neck, standing an inch or so taller.

"Igu!" I said loudly. "Here I am!"

Igu's eyes rolled about the room. Then he threw his head back and took a swig from a whisky bottle. Was that mine? Two barebodied ex-prize fighters stood either side of him. The three of them stood over the tall counter from which they ran the thriving establishment. There had been rumors in the air ever since I could remember that the two toughs had got their permanent bloodshot eyes behind bars.

A sudden dimness descended; there has never been mistaking when the light goes out even in the glare of a single fluorescent. Nor when my stomach turns into open revolt.

Igu finally set his eyes in my direction. It was hard, unusual; but my anger, still mercurial, was equal to the moment. I stretched out my right palm and took a step forward.

"Back to your books, young man, go!" he cried hoarsely, "this life is not for you." I could hardly recognize his voice, could hardly believe him. Instead I saw the University registrar withdrawing his proffered hand of acceptance. I could hear the cackle of Benji and the other boys, Chief Haw-Haw's sneer. I could see the contempt on Enene's face. But why had Igu done this to me? Evidently he was drunk now.

Another step, my arms still outstretched. eyes dark red, yet. One more step and the two men shot upright, ramrod like machine-gadgets. I halted. I didn't like the way the muscles on their bared arms rose and fell like the tides of a rising storm.

Sudden laughter erupted everywhere at this precise moment. Even more suddenly I noticed there were other bottles of whisky and wine and beer littered all over the place. "April fool! April for fools!" The bawdy cries were meant for me to hear. I then noticed three others behind me, the continuing puzzle in their eyes unmistakable. April the first — Fools Day — how could I have forgotten? Yes, Igu Eweka had a sense of humor indeed, humor of sorts. Everyone did.

The ladies at the office who talked all day long. Government officials who plan all year long to no end. My landlord who treated life like some running joke — I shuddered at the prospects of his waiting at my door, with the crowd of fellow tenants, all awaiting my return with the promised gold and silver. How they would haw-haw at me. My stomach turned every which way as I kept counting the cost of these ninety minutes past. April for fools. Yes — I ought to burst out laughing, but I couldn't. Something choked me. There are a person's finest hours; this was my oddest. I began to leave.

No, I wouldn't want to meet Enene either. Not until all this settles down, then perhaps, I might tell her about this wicked trick... Or, perhaps, about the wages of dreams without controls... But I had no choice in the matter: Right outside, in the fast-gathering darkness, away from the lamp posts, Enene stood waving! I had virtually succeeded in turning tail — for she had been looking slightly away — when she called me and came over. We met at the doorway, the chuckling crowd behind me.

One look at my face and she burst out laughing too. "Why take these people serious?" She asked as we walked down the crowded street. Why take dreams too seriously, I reframed her words. I had no answer, really. Aloud I said, "It was all a joke."

"April the first?" she said more to herself, then aloud to me, yet in a conspiratorial tone, "I knew there was a joke somewhere — it never fails to happen on this day, you know." Then she told me of how her next-door neighbor had woken her at four-thirty to say her father was out by the street, on an urgent visit — and how the other tenants had had a laugh at the ensuing anxiety as she rushed out. At that, I managed to chuckle.

Her light chatter transformed me, I can say this now. That night Enene and I went with Benji to watch *The Guns of Iva Valley*, the first of many such trips in the days ahead, but I couldn't have known it then.

In retrospect, I could say the sun had kept its promise.

# The Engineering Dean's Tale

It nearly came

to pass that the glory of putting the first man in space almost didn't go to the Russian Yuri Gagarin, but to the tiny central European principality Strassetat. In hindsight, it is even more remarkable that Strassetat lost its historic chance to bubble among the top ranks of the world's Space Age powers because of an old malaise that psychiatrists would later think of as a form of social dementia.

The story began that day in the late 1950s, a few years before the flight of the Soyuz, but after the first spacecraft — similarly named but differently numbered — had taken the first living creature into space, the poor heroic dog Laika; that was back in 1957.

It was graduation day at the Strassetat State University.

Okey Ezeri was known to everyone by his boyhood nickname O. K. Kinkana. O. K. the Kicker, it really was; Kicker had quickly become kinkana after the strong home-brew whiskey that gave even the bravest a knotted kick in the stomach. The other boys in the Stella Marris secondary school soccer team were sure he would one day play for the famed Port Harcourt Red Devils. Then he had won one of those scholarships to Europe for bright people in colonies on the verge of independence. The nickname had stuck with him even in Strassetat where the other undergraduates found it easier to mouth. Now years later, he was the only black man in the huge auditorium. Front and back, rising high, rows of curving seats contained only white men and women. In the next hour or so, it would be over for all of them there, and people would begin to move on to other things.

Okey looked down at the podium where the assembled dignitaries, deans, and full professors were seated. He noticed the powerful chairman of the University Council of Strassetat, the State Parliamentary Chief Whip, lazily fanning himself with a folded paper, his wife beside him. The Chairman of the Academic Council, Enzo Enrique, that maverick of nuclear research, stood before the lectern reading an address to the graduating class.

Okey thought of the long, rough road from the dusty schools of the working class Port Harcourt district of Diobu to those of the sedate "reserved areas" of the old European Quarter. But like most other youngsters in those days, one treat stood out the most: the trips to the new Kingsway shopping mall in the city center, with its chain escalators bearing one through several floors of sparkling merchandise in a thousand colors! For him the early promise of a soccer career, of a destiny for great things ahead, provided now only moments of prideful reflection, even as he wondered what future lay for a nuclear engineer. How far away he had come from that initial direction! He would never forget the day the coach named him the youngest soccer maestro destined to succeed the legendary ones,

Thunder Balogun and Onyeanwuna the Master Dribbler, of how he would one day be in the red uniform of the Red Devils to face their great nemesis, the dreaded Giant Killers of Aba. But he had made a distinction pass when the West African School Certificate Examinations results came out and then the scholarships. Now as he sat watching the annual ritual, he thought of the great loneliness of this land of energetic but distant people, with their rains and snow and low-key, understated politics. Yes, he had waited long for this day, the day after which he would be free to take a giant step in shaping his real life as a scientist in Africa's race to catch up and move past the rest. Before him loomed the image of home, lush greens, and dancing maidens, land with an assured rhythm of life stretching millennia. It would be quite a change after all this time. He found the thought flowing through his mind: Guard jealously, Africa, guard those eternal norms that might be buffeted away by an imported culture on the mistaken belief that foreign was finest....But talk was but that. They of this generation that must be pioneers and pathfinders, they must set forth in broad energetic steps to recreate a civilization that for half a millennium was in eclipse. Today he was taking a tiny step, which, joined with others here and there, would start the stream of change on its fated course. Yes, there would be much to do for a scientist who was also a cultural nationalist.

He lit a cigarette and puffed smoke. The girl sitting beside him twitched her nose and looked away. He puffed again and again, thinking of the endless challenges ahead once he returned to Nigeria. The Pan-Africanist ideals of the new Ghana premier Kwame Nkrumah appealed very much to him: a united Africa capable of mobilizing its vast but truncated resources, human and physical, and roaring up to the peacocked powers of today. He would be part of making that happen; like many others in the various universities in

London and Paris, Brussels and Madrid, Bonn and Geneva, Moscow and Washington, he knew his was the age that had that rendez-vous with destiny the ancients had long spoken of. Home, sweet home and the work to be done!

The time finally came, and Okey Ezeri stepped down to collect his academic insignia. Climbing up to the podium before the grand chancellor in his red-lined purple robes and gold-rimmed broad hat, he bowed stiffly but felt most elated. It was all over at last. Scattered applause greeted the lone foreigner from another world. Let that other nagging question of what he would be doing back home with a degree in nuclear engineering wait.

-II-

Okey came out of the huge auditorium an hour later. A mild sun met his face, and the wind rustled his clothes. The pines swayed and whistled. The well-paved road glistened. He would take a taxi for today. This was a special day, not one for buses. So he waited.

A car pulled up, surprising him. It was a Jaguar, a woman at the wheel.

"Hello!" she called, leaning out. "Are you O. K. Kinkana?"

Puzzled, he took a step back from the curb. "Yes," he answered without smiling — why should he? "I am O. K. Kinkana."

"Off to your place?"

"Yes"

"Waiting for transport?"

"Yes."

"Care if I give you a ride?"

"Not if you can."

"Oh," she laughed. "I'll be glad to. Come on in."

He stepped in through the front door she had opened for him.

The seat was soft and comfortable.

"I'm Tina," she said.

"You already know me," he observed.

"Of course, you are Kinkana. Is that a first or second name?"

"Full name is Okey Ezeri. Everyone calls me O. K. Kinkana."

"Oh, how beautiful!" she laughed.

"You think so?"

"Oh, sure. Sounds easier than Dr. Okey Ezeri." She pronounced both names the way most Europeans would: E-z-e-r-y rather than E-z-e-ree, without the right inflection, Okey like Oakey.

"Tell me — who are you?" They had met at a party last Christmas, she said, and had spent a while talking to each other. Didn't he remember? He couldn't. They drove on in silence. He lived in a quiet neighborhood, three miles from the university. From the look of things, she could even have known his destination. So he refrained from asking her if she did. He was always cautious about those who knew him more than he did them.

He half-turned toward her. It had happened once in a while that someone gave him a ride, but it had most often been a man. And the gaiety of this lady — he put her age at twenty-three or so — made him feel a bit jittery,

Quite a pretty one, though — her turtle-neck, her eternal smile, her bright, wide eyes, and her incessant chatter on trivialties. She was wearing slacks of a fine material held by a belt. Long legs. He wasn't sure what to make of her.

The city was now behind them; they were on the wide double-carriage autobahn. Tina let the car fly. Okey said nothing. She had stopped chattering and seemed to concentrate on managing the ever-increasing speed. The houses and apple trees on the side flashed past like a fast-forward motion picture. Apples grew like grass in

Strassetat. He tried to light a cigarette; the light blew off. She brought out a glowing lighter from the car without saying anything. He took it from her, lit and puffed, then gave the lighter back to her.

"In a hurry?" he asked casually.

"You don't like speed?" she quizzed, laughing.

"I didn't say that."

"But you imply it."

"Well, yes. I don't like speed."

"I am sorry." She slowed down. "Mind if I ask?"

"What?"

"My place is just nearby. Come and have a glass of Crintage on me."

"Thank you. Why, if I may ask?"

"But, you've just graduated."

"Yes -"

"Making one of the best results in the Faculty."

"I hardly think that matters. How did you get to know?"

"I work at the Faculty of Technology."

"But I've never seen you before."

"Don't be ridiculous," she laughed. "You can't have known everyone of the two hundred and ten administrative staff."

"Well, Tina, I think I'd like to go home."

"Oh, now that's nonsense, Okey. If it's about my husband, I'm still a spinster." She looked at him and laughed.

Okey felt heartened. The seat now felt rather hot; he shifted uncomfortably. A party had been arranged for him by his kindly landlady, to which the cream of the town had been invited. Even the maverick himself, who had taken him in Nuclear Engineering, named Enzo Enrique, professor and Nobel Prize laureate of '48, Chairman of Strassetat Board of Space Research, was to be there. It was a closely guarded secret that they were working for the first manned space ship but progress was yet vague. Okey had worked as a research assistant in his first year. Professor Enrique would give a toast at the party; he would say something about how the future always belonged to those with a sense of mission, of destiny, of the will to tough it out, daring and ducking. Strange man, this Enrique. Captured by the Nazis while at a conference in Paris — some said he was actually an eager volunteer, having assisted the team that almost perfected Hitler's Secret Weapon, the V-Rocket, and escaping just in time before the Americans and the Russians scrambled to lay their hands on them, rather their brains, for their own space program.

Okey would have to get to his place soon. This was his night. The township was called Villaburg. Its inhabitants counted a comfortable middle class who did everything to maintain Villaburg's reputation as a respectable suburb. This tiny country was a strange enough outpost of Europe. Over the decades, it had maintained a self-imposed isolation and neutrality in world politics; the then ruler of Strassetat, King Francisco Hapsburg Niccqo III, had declared that his little Kingdom belonged to whites and whites alone. All non-whites — reds, browns, and blacks — had accordingly been flushed out.

Upon his overthrow in 1932, his republican successors, apart from maintaining their isolation even against the dreaded Hitler and the subtle machinations of the Allies, had also contrived to keep all non-white races, especially blacks, out of the little Republic. But Hitler's racist excesses and the post-war moves towards internationalism made this overtly impossible — why, it was the age of foreign aid as well, of extending hands to the 'little brown brothers' in the Southern Hemisphere. Strassetat thus joined other European states in this reluctant effort, having joined the United Nations in 1948.

By 1950, Strassetat had become fairly advanced, industrialized. And upon his arrival, the new generation, not used to seeing blacks, accorded Okey Ezeri, the honor of a strange wonder from across the seas. Not even the impression written in archaic books that witches and wizards were black and that it was to Africa that God had first hauled Satan and Beelzebub could make the curious, independent-minded republicans fail to admire the quiet dignity and carriage of Kinkana the African. He was also a student to be reckoned with, as his fellows related.

"So what do you say?" asked Tina.

There was something about this girl. Well, if she was so keen, so what? He was not one to refuse an invitation that might lead to a long-term relationship.

"Lead the way then," he said in a level voice. "Could stay a moment for a drink."

-III-

The house seemed big and empty, despite from the elaborate furniture, rugs, mahogany tables, sofas, glass balls, hanging balloons, and oriental curtains. Large pictures of gilded military characters with scowling faces hung from the walls; it was all so quiet.

He flipped through a magazine, waiting for her. She returned carrying two tall glasses.

"Crintage," she said sitting down.

"Cheers!" She sat down next to him. They drank slowly in silence, their bodies touching. "Cheers!" he replied spiritedly, warming to her friendship.

"I understand they are having a party for you tonight," she said.

"Who told you?"

She laughed. "Oh, well, I get to hear things, you know."

"A spy would do well in your position then."

She seemed startled. "Isn't that a dirty job."

"I am hearing that for the first time," he remarked drily.

"How do you mean?"

"How could a Westerner say such a thing? Spying is a respected way of life among you Europeans. Where I come from, your trust and honor is not lightly — "

She patted him, laughing. "It's a necessity among us, you know. Leave that aside. Let's talk about the party."

"Well, let's talk about it."

"I'd like to be there."

"It's open, I think."

She sipped her drink. He looked at her and felt he was beginning to like her. There was a certain abandon about her that he found attractive.

"When are you leaving for Africa?"

"A week's time."

"So soon?"

"So soon," he said. "I am homesick."

"You've been here six years."

"Sure."

"But you would come back?"

"What for?"

"Just to see us for instance."

He recognized his seeming ingratitude at once. "Of course, of course. But now I have some important things I want to do in Africa."

"Like?"

"Oh, lots of things. Let's forget all about that, can we?"

"Oh, why not."

Again the friendly silence. She had a permanent smile on her face, like a nice teenager. They both finished their drinks.

"Are you going by air or sea?" She was back on the subject.

"Ship — the Black Star Line."

"Black Star?"

"Belongs to Ghana, the new republic back home in Africa. You've heard of the leader, Kwame Nkrumah?"

"He's a radical, isn't he?"

"Well, he is first and foremost, a visionary."

"Is he any good?"

"He's great." He stood up. "Time to go."

"Have you seen my art collection yet?" Tina asked.

He started and paused. He often remembered the stories told of a certain gold mask removed from the face of the statue of the High God Dim in his very village a hundred years ago by white traders. Who knows? The treasure might be lying in some basement somwehere in Europe or hanging in some young heiresse's Manhattan condo.

Taking him firmly by the arm, Tina went along the inner passage. She was talking as she went. "My father was a surgeon in the English colonies years ago. It was from there that he collected all the art treasure he left me and my mother. You know I was an only child. We stayed back in Europe while he went out there and caught some unnameable disease. There was no cure. For years he lingered on, then passed away one cold night. Mom caught the disease too and died a year after. I am all that's left, me and this house. It's all I've got."

Okey muttered how terrible. She stopped before a door which

she threw open. An exquisite bedroom draped in oriental make-up spread before him.

"Your bedroom?"

"Yes. It's here. Step in."

He stepped in. With one deft movement Tina slammed the door close and slipped the key into her trouser pockets.

Okey looked at her. "What's the game?" he asked. His mind was working fast. Overpower her at once. He was not afraid of her even if she were armed.

"Okey," she whispered, unzipping. "I want you. Undress. Quick." In a moment, her own clothing was off; she wore no underpants. Her soft nakedness made him blink.

Okey blinked again. "With all pleasure," he said slowly, not hearing the tiny bells ringing in his ears.

-IV-

Professor Enrique arrived on time. Tina met him at the front door. She opened it, and he stepped forward into the house smartly.

"Is he alright?" he asked, pecking her lips.

"Yes, honey. He passed out," she said.

"How long ago?"

"About thirty minutes."

The professor was a tall man by any standards. His pointed beard and mustache, fashionable in Strassetat, along with his pince-nez resting complacently at the bridge of his nose gave him a tinge of the absent-minded but sharp-eyed academic — which was exactly what he was.

Professor Enrique shrugged off his thin-lapeled coat; he was now dressed only in a pink shirt and broad short tie. "Let's see him," he said.

Once inside the room the two stopped abruptly as if by some mechanism. He saw the decanters.

"You used this?"

"I used Crintage." she laughed.

"Good. Then there was no need for the bedroom?"

"There was no need for it?"

"Sure."

"Don't be silly, Enzo."

He bent and kissed her. She responded fully, and they held on to each other for some time. When next he tried to speak, his voice was a little hoary. She understood and began to reach for him. But he quickly recovered.

"Pity he can't go to his party tonight," he said reflectively.

"Pity," she said, looking into his eyes.

"Alright," the professor snapped suddenly and lifted Tina off her feet and went through the passage and kicked open the bedroom door. He saw the body sprawled face-up on the floor.

"Ha! What's this? Why is he in your — ?"

"Silly!" Tina jumped down from him. "You didn't even ask me where he was."

Enrique rapped his forehead. "I am always like this with you."

"Yes, because you always want me first."

Enzo Enrique turned a little red. "Ah, don't say such things, Tina."

They quickly undressed.

-V-

The Chancellor stood at attention as the martial music played softly. In the distance the sound of sea water splashing on the rocky shores provided a background to the solemn and yet internationally eventful occasion. But for one thing — it was supposed to be a top state secret.

Few people among the whole of Strassetat's one million inhabitants knew about this moment. This was the finale of "Operation Moonbound," which would become known to history as "The Great Near-Miss," for in the next few days the world would be taken by surprise. The planners knew the four powers would be the most astounded — and offended. Definitely the British MI-5, the American CIA, and the Russian KGB would all come under severe criticism for not uncovering the secret of a mere one million people inhabiting one of the tiniest states on earth. But the problem had always been its neutrality. Though a member of the United Nations, Strassetat had consistently refrained from bloc voting and joined progressive movements — East as well as West, North and South — without stepping on the ideological toes of the superpowers. In this sense Strassetatians preferred to think of themselves as being like the Swiss without the self-serving neutrality.

Yes. It would all go as planned. The Big Powers needed to be reminded from time to time that the other name for the Space Age was the Age of the Push Button, that the issue was not size but technological preeminence. Why, one of the foremost weapons experts had spoken of Fortress Strassetat ringed with nuclear-tipped missiles on mobile launchers and of satellites in outer space programmed to guard against enemy dart missiles. Something that fanciful — but that went to tell: It would be brain over brawn from now on!

Now those in the know could feel it all about them, this race into the history books: Strassetat would swing into the big news in the next few weeks. There was, of course, the other side of it, for surely Strassetat could become the center of international intrigue between East and West. The whole world would insist that Strassetat declare its stand, and cease its fence-sitting antics. They would insist; they would seek to coerce Strassetat. But that would be but the beginning of a series of dazzling technological breakthroughs this gifted land would spring on the rest of the world — for a purpose that would be clear when the time was right and ripe.

The leaders were confident enough that if they could withstand the next few weeks, wriggle out of the tightrope certain to be thrown in their path, the rest would be easier. Why, it had been so in the past when Strassetat outmaneuvered the Triple Entente and the Triple Alliance powers of the First All-European World War of the twentieth century. Strassetat had maintained its bluff against the Axis and the Allied powers in the second. It was keeping out of the Cold War. It would keep out of the space rivalry. No one even knew that the tiny state of ingenious people had also invented the atom and the hydrogen bombs much about the same time the proud powers were exploding theirs. But of its own free will the Etat, the supreme representative organ of the people, vetoed further experimentation on nuclear armaments.

The Chancellor took the salute. He was an old man in a white bemedalled marshall's uniform. Enrique hugged him. "I will be back," he said. The men behind the Chancellor smiled and nodded appreciatively.

The Chancellor had not spoken. He kept looking at the professor. Finally, he murmured, "You will come back with honors for the fatherland."

Enrique bowed. The small group of ministers and generals of

The Engineering Dean's Tale

the police cheered; Strassetat had no army.

The martial music struck up. There was a light moon but no electric light. At the beach the huge space ship loomed in the night. A group of scientists and technicians waited at its base.

As the group began to walk towards the beach, Tina emerged and slipped into the arms of the professor. None of the others said anything. They had protested in vain that the woman should not go. But Enrique had insisted on the grounds of the advancement of science. There was, for one thing, the unsolved Darwinian riddle on the species; when it came to humans, a number of things are yet to be resolved. Left to him, he argued, he would have had red and brown persons accompany him on this trip so as to test something in Gobineau's works on the subject of race and human progress; he had his own notions as well to flesh out once there. The cause of science must be advanced as national power marches on. But the Etat Ministerial Council was firm. The woman, maybe, but no one else. This had cost so much money, and the glory of hoisting the nation to the pinnacle often reserved for neighboring Switzerland must not be jeopardized by this premature quest; maybe next time around, but this time, Strassetat would be another little mouse that roared. The Minister of Propaganda, who had given the final knockout speech, was a master of imagery in his own right. But that was in vain; Enrique, stubborn as the honorable minister was eloquent, had an answer to those who would stop the march of science. Even now, to the very ship they were walking towards, inside the very spaceship that had drained several million etates, lay the limp form of the fresh African Ph.D., unconscious among the food packages.

Beside the spaceship, the group stopped. Enrique pressed a button, and the latch flew open, yielding a stepladder. The martial music struck up once more, and Enrique and Tina stood at attention.

Smartly he raised his hand and touched his cap.

The Chancellor said: "A most unique moment in the long history of our glorious nation. We'll take a photograph for remembrance."

They began to line up, the ministers and the generals. The technicians, too, would take a photograph with him. The glory of the moment! This was Prof. Enrique's hour, destined to last long enough to pass into history.

-VI-

As the group approached the spaceship, Okey woke with a start. It was dark, and he did not know where he was from the first word. His mind grew alert rather quickly, and he tried to piece the issues together. Yes, Tina's house. Her naked body. The lovemaking... ah, that had been good. Yes. What next? What next? He could remember nothing more. Everything had gone blank after the lovemaking. Certainly the drink must have been drugged and timed.

His eyes had become used to the darkness. He realized that he must be lying in a square object — maybe a carton box or something similar. Then for the first time he became aware of the objects resting on him. Instinctively he fumbled with his fingers upwards and felt. It was hard going alright, but he soon established that those must be fruits of some sort. Probably apples. Gradually he forced his arm up through the fruits. Then he felt some cloth or other soft material. What was the meaning of all this? His hand rose through into free atmosphere. Whatever it was lying on top of him seemed like it could be moved. His heart began to beat wildly. Could it be that he had been left at a deserted spot — possibly with a time bomb waiting to go off? How much time did he have? Or could it be he was on his way to some place he would not wish to go? Maybe right now in some vehicle boot? He listened. There was no sound of anything in motion, only muffled voices nearby. He decided that he was at a spot. Once more panic overtook him. He had to act fast. It might be that he had only seconds left!

Opposed by the weight above him and the smallness of the compartment in which he lay, with a heave and a final energetic effort, Okey rose head first. The apples clattered down; he blinked. The place was well lit.

Quickly he scrambled out of the box, a wooden box, he noticed. He looked around. A control board of red and blue gadgets, two compartments to the left, one containing a seat, the other a bed; a glass view-hole, wall compass, lighting controls; the communications gadgets, the cartographic materials, the guns, knives and food items — he took all these in with a quick, comprehending glance.

Now Okey knew he was in the Strasse Moon vehicle — (SMV-60) — the space ship whose existence he only knew of from the paper model he had helped Enrique construct! With a shudder, he immediately understood why he was here. The term guinea pig passed through his mind's eye more than figuratively. He was quite aware of the professor's predilection with racial superiority and inferiority theories and all that.

Well, he had to do something. For one, he knew how to disable the ship. He fell on the gadgets with a vengeance.

-VIII-

Minutes later, outside, the Chancellor and his ministers and generals stepped back. The pictures were done; it was time to let history take its course, to let the world stretch the story from the pyramid-building Egyptians to the bridge-building Persians of the

Peloponnesian Wars through the engineering of the Romans and their timeless highways down through Michelangelo's designs and the technological wonder of the Wright Brothers. Then there would be the "Enzo Enrique Breakthrough." The Nobel Prize for sure....

Enrique and Tina climbed gingerly up the ladder and through the latch. He pressed a button, and the ladder shot out of view into its place.

Heads bobbing out, the two waved at those below; the latter waved back and cheered.

"Fine!" cried the professor. At once their heads disappeared, and the latch shut close. The technicians began quickly to gather around. They had only two minutes to shoot SVC-60 and commence Operation Moonbound.

Meanwhile, a few kilometers away, the Chancellor and his entourage were discussing the political consequences of this night's event.

"We've beaten the Americans," said one minister. "We've beaten the Russians to it! Permit me to say, sir, that this mighty principality may well have taken its first step in the grand order of human destiny."

"They are supposed to launch theirs when?" someone asked.

"Tomorrow," came the reply.

"Precisely at first light — in five hours."

"The Chancellor, sir, I believe, would make the broadcast to the world this very night about this great achievement." It was the Info-Prop Minister who spoke.

"Of course," said the Chancellor of Strassetat waving a sheet of papers. "You have taken care of my speech?"

"As always, Your Excellency. And the SBC has been informed to stand by for a most important occasion in an hour's time," an aide informed them.

"We are going to take the world by surprise," the Minister rejoiced.

The Chancellor nodded. "It is time Strassetat took its place as a power on this planet. Numbers have nothing to do with it, only intelligence and the will to dare, as Nietzsche might have put it."

"What's keeping these people?" asked the Army General suddenly.

They looked at the group of scientists and technicians in the distance. No action. The space ship was still where it was. The leader of the team cried, "Ready! Fire!" several times but each time nothing happened. A man began to cry.

Suddenly the latch flew open, and Professor Enrique's head shot out, dishevelled, eyes blazing. A single word rang out from him: "Sabotage!"

The notables looked at one another. The CIA or the KGB. Who else? Instinctively, they all began to make for the spaceship at a trot, swearing.

-IX-

Villaburg. People's patience had been stretched to the limit. The party that the landlady and hostess of the evening had sent out to see if "her" black had had an accident came back with no such news.

Then why had he not yet come back? Guests had been around for almost an hour, and many were already thinking of going home.

"Maybe he doesn't like our company," suggested the local member of the Etat. He was to chair the occasion. His massive frame dominated the high table with the curved bottles of Crintage and Champagne, the chandeliers and a small set of fireworks. Balloons splashed brightly in the colors of the rainbow floated gently to and fro — from the ceiling.

There were about twenty leading citizens of the small town gathered in the compact living room. One or two were millionaires, two lectured at the Villaburg Polytechnic, where Okey had taken his first degree. Others from the representative at the Etat, were middle-class stock brokers, savvy media types and lawyers, and one was a medical doctor, his wife, a nurse, clinging to his arm. Even Enrique, who was supposed to read a citation to his pupil from the Strassetat Friends of Africa Society, was nowhere yet.

It seemed the party was a failure, and there was nothing the poor hostess could do other than declare it so and save people their time.

The hostess rose, and cleared her voice. Her mind was made up. She had not gone beyond the first words when the curtains swung open, and Okey strode in. The party gave him a half-warm ovation. He was well-dressed, scented, with a flower on the lapel of his fine coat. He looked supremely comely — and not a few of the younger men were forced to mute their initial enthusiasm, nervously looking at the women's eyes for reassurance. They had also heard of those stories about black men's sexuality, though some woman who knew better, having been in Germany during the Occupation, said it was all myth.

"African time!" joked someone. "Sorry, I am so sorry, but this has nothing to do with African time," he beamed. "See, as I was coming down, I ran across an accident victim who had passed out in the midst of crates of apples and Crintage." He knew this didn't make sense to them, but he went on quickly. "I've been at the hospital all day. I am sorry. So sorry everyone — unavoidably delayed!"

The gathering heartily forgave him. The hostess began to bustle, and everyone began to settle once more, a happy gaiety on. He went from one couple to the other.

Five minutes later, Okey walked up to the hostess and whispered, "Just one moment, ma'am; I have someone — I think from the hospital, waiting outside. I'll be back." And he was gone, not just from the party. A taxi was waiting for him. The station was not far off; a train left in the next seven minutes. O. K. Kinkana was in the 11:30 run to the border, heading for Switzerland. From there he would take a plane to Ghana, then to Lagos, Nigeria. Africa at last! He had won his freedom by escaping through a secret latch while the confusion was going on below. He had tumbled stealthily into the water, swam and waded for half a mile, then walked through the bushes to the road. A kindly old couple gave him a ride. He had reached his apartment, freshened up, threw a few things together, summoned a taxi, and gone over to his landlady's, next door, for the party.

-X-

When finally Strassetat recovered and prepared to go on with Operation Moonbound, it was too late. The Russians launched the Sputnik a few hours later that same day, and a heartbroken Enrique killed himself with an overdose of spiked Crintage. It finally emerged however that the CIA, too, had an inkling after all. The kidnapping of the young African doctorate gave them time to confirm and warn Washington — which swung into action at once. Somehow, despite her neutrality, Strassetat did not seek to second the USSR.

*****

Okey Ezeri once more looked across an auditorium. It was years and years later, and he was now Dean of the School of Engineering at the University of Nigeria, Nsukka. He, Dr. Okey Ezeri, presiding over the launching of the Africa Space-Probe Lab! His story, briefer than the foregoing, more pungent, with all the immediacy of the terror of the kidnapped guinea pig, had brought the audience at the Princess Alexandria Hall to its feet. Then the distinguished audience of grandees, officials, students, and journalists held their breath as the grand old man of Nigerian politics, Nnamdi Azikiwe, rose to make a donation of a hundred thousand or so, insisting that Africa's quest must begin while he still breathed. As the assembled spirits soared high at the aged legend's gesture and the new Taiwan-Tokyo-New York import-export magnates reached for their checkbooks, the Dean knew he must keep the stories going. History must be used in the service of the future. The time had come to be at the vanguard, just as it had been a few thousand years back, starting from Ancient Khemet and Axum, Kush and Meroe....

To Tangle With Tarzan

When all

of a sudden that day in late June, her name rang out, Rosie jerked forward, petrified. In the next instant Bobby, her cousin, was hugging her. She had no idea she would win the new travel prize. She had no idea that of the over one hundred and five kids who had entered for the K. O. Dike Student Exchange Prize Contest for Boston high school seniors and juniors, she might be the lucky one. Rosie, a junior, had merely entered an essay on how the myriad cultures of the world had as many similarities as they had differences.

The prize announcement had taken place in the Boston Charles High School auditorium that fine June day, Graduation and Prize Day. A large hall of one thousand capacity, it would be filled with hopeful seniors and juniors and their families. It was a Sunday afternoon and people had been seated by three o' clock, more or less. They had started arriving a little before two — the young people first. Some had drifted in from church services. There was Mark Johnson, the black boy who now was one of the seniors about to graduate. There was Bennett Thomas, half Anglo and half Italian, whose mother was said to be a distant cousin of one of those royalties England still kept in place. He, too, was a senior. Now and then he threw a glance to where Rosie and three other girls giggled animatedly about something or other.

    Presently the principal appeared on the balcony of the second floor where the administrative offices were housed. And in his great voice that carried through the entire courtyard to the parking lot, he bellowed: "Time!" Everyone immediately began to drift toward the Assembly Hall. They filed in by ones and twos. Old Mr. Bonaparte Danzig stood by the door, as impressive in his tuxedo as ever. Everyone knew his story. He had fled the Nazis in the thirties, travelling across Europe before coming to the States. Mastering English in a year of manic determination, he had gone into teaching, rising over the past three decades to his present exalted status. It was said one of his ancestors had been a full imperial officer under Napoleon and had actually ridden into Germany beside the ambitious French emperor, whose white stallion and flowing robes had left such an impression on Kant and the other enlightened German philosophes, those afficianodos of progress, who had seen in him more than the age promised. Ever since then a member of the Danzig family had always had a name from that period — even in faraway America. Bonaparte Danzig's only daughter was named Josephine; his brother's sons were in turn named Philip and Ferdinand.
"Great day, Mark!" he said cheerfully to the black youth whose admission in '76 had caused such a furor; it was the era of the violent anti-busing violent demonstrations at City Hall.

    "Yeah," smiled the young man, aware of the significance of the day.″Sure, Mr. Danzig — and thanks for everything."

He also beamed at Rosie Sharon as she came up with her uncle.

"Hi, Mr. Danzig," she said.

"Nice day, m'dear. Looking forward to the prizes, huh?"

"Yes and no!" quipped the sixteen year old.

"Oh, I know," laughed Mr. Danzig. "Prom night is on your mind."

Rosie waved and entered the huge auditorium and threaded her way to where her proud relatives were already seated, according to an alphabetical seating arrangement. And an hour later she heard her name: Rosie Sharon Baxter, Exchange Prize to Nigeria. More formally, the Kenneth Dike Student Exchange Prize for Inter-Cultural Understanding. For what seemed like an eternity, all she could hear was the clapping. Her cousin gave her a bear-hug, and Uncle Zed patted her back and shook hands — he was always the formal one even in moments like this.

Then she stepped forward to receive the envelope. It was as if her feet were on springs, as if unseen hands propelled her forward, made her smile and curtsey as she accepted the prize certificate; it was as if something guided her back to her seat. A legendary figure in his homeland, Kenneth Dike, she had long known, was the Nigerian professor of history at Harvard whose coming — as the prize originator, Ebo Maduka, Ph.D., would explain in an interview with the Boston Globe — had meant a lot to the small Africanist community at the great institution.

-II-

Ed Wagner stood at a corner of the auditorium, microphone in hand and fed the Channel 7 evening news network. The K. O. Dike Prize had been announced and sixteen year-old Rosie Sharon Baxter is the winner. Presently the young woman appeared before Boston's half-million TV viewers. Yes, she was thrilled. Yes, she would go to Africa. Indeed, she looked forward to it. Oh, yes, she had heard of the place. Well, not learnt much of it really. Oh, yes, Idi Amin — everyone has heard of Idi Amin. Nkrum. . . mah? Azikiwe? No, never heard of those. Nyere? No? Bogie and Kate Hepburn in *the African Queen*? Yes, seen that. What impressed me? Oh, the lions, the rhinos, the waterfalls, and the wilds. True nature, huh? Yes. Giggle. Tarzan? Oh, yes, yes — Tarzan of the Apes. The last movie — what's it called? *The Legend of Tarzan*. Yes, seen that too. Oh, seen a lot of Tarzans. Read most of the series. Yeah? Well, you know everyone's waiting for the new release, *Tangling With Tarzan* — greatest story ever told. Saw the preview myself. Tarzan of the Apes, Lord Greystoke.

Ed caught himself just in time to stop the impromptu promotion. Of course, everyone had been waiting for the sequel to the highly successful *Legend*, and he needn't push the fact that like everyone else, he was no less delirious with anticipation. Just a few more days.

Leaving in three weeks? Good luck. Thanks.

"Well, before we say, 'Hello Africa, here comes a Bostonian,' let's try a little quiz for our young Africa traveller." Ed Wagner paused for a moment, then popped a flat one: "Where is Lagos?" He held his piece of paper rather importantly.

"You got to be joking," said the prize winner, starting.

"No, I am not. Do you know how many people don't know in

which direction Oregon is, much less Africa? So tell our viewers where Lagos is?"

"Lagos — but that's where I'd be going."

"Okay, so you know that. Where is Nairobi?"

"Kenya."

"And Dar es Salaam?"

"Capital of Tanzania."

He looked into his paper. "And Kaduna?"

"Also in Nigeria."

"Enugu?"

"Nigeria, I think. Do you mind if I pop one at you, Ed?" asked Rosie."Where is Khartoum?"

"South Africa," he replied.

"No!" Rosie cried."Zambia, I think."

"Zanzibar — who knows!" They both burst out laughing. It sounded like, Who cares? "This makes the point, folks. They should make geography compulsory again," observed Ed Wagner signing off.

Rosie saw Ed Wagner's report on TV that night. They had come back early from the barbecue hosted by the principal for the various prize winners, sixteen all told. It had taken place in the back yard of his handsome Lexington home, where he and his wife, five years older and showing it, had lived for years. Their only child, Shereen, a thirty-five year old nurse and still single, had been on hand to play the piano from the second floor balcony: She had been good at it, wafting enchanting tunes of "America the Beautiful" and "This Land Is My Land, This Land Is Your Land." The parents had gathered below the balcony to watch the pianist, clapping wistfully when a crescendo turned into a diminuendo. They had joined her when she began the national anthem. The old headmaster, at first bent over at the other end of the large garden scooping hamburgers and chicken breasts from the barbecue grill, had straightened himself as the tunes wafted across, then stood erect, ramrod. The crowd of young prize winners had followed in imitation. And following the last strain upon which the parents and relatives and visitors had broken into a cheer, they had fallen eagerly on the sizzling provisions on the grill.

Later that evening, Rosie and Bobby, his parents Zed and Tracey Hubbard, all would look up from the television evening news at the same time as her interview with Wagner ended. "Not bad," granted Uncle Zed. In his forties, he was heavy-set construction foreman with a neck that resembled a bull's and never one for many words. He had taken custody of his niece after the tragedy because it was simply the right thing to do, though in these more hedonistic times that was looking more and more old-fashioned. And he had not regretted it so far: She had become a sister to his son Bobby and had made her way into the prestigious Boston E, as everyone called the school. If only those integration fights had come out the other way...

"Better than that," interjected his wife, "it was a sterling performance. I always thought Rose Sharon would be an actress some day." Tracey Hubbard was a good-looking woman for her forty years. She and Zed had met in Dorchester High, class of '61, and had been married right after graduation. She had improved her typing, gone for bookkeeping courses, and ever since supplemented the family income with a job as a BayBank teller. They had bought the house at Cabot Lodge Place back in '69, a full sixteen years ago. She and Zed still shook their heads in honest wonder at what had happened to the real estate market, how in a mere decade-and-half a good three-bedroom house had gone from twenty to one hundred and twenty thousand, even when average income, for those who followed these things, had climbed from six to only twelve thousand. The economic forecasters said to blame it on inflation, brought on by those Arabs and their Texan friends in the oil business and by that generation who were once called Baby Boomers and now Yuppies. Like a tribe of monkeys with a herd instinct, they had all moved into high tech and fat paychecks, to the delight of real estate agents and landlords, who kept stretching the limits of the free marketplace. Not even the half-hearted entry of state and municipal authorities into the housing market with their rent-control programs could help the scores of thousands who came of age into a situation where the first beneficiaries proved to be permanent renters.

"But Mom, don't you think Rosie nearly overdid the reverse interview bit?" asked Bobby, sinking into a yellow Florida apple. "Did you see Ed tighten?"

"No, I did not," said Rosie defensively, "I should have asked him more. He was pump-priming me. He could have made a total fool of me."

"I think it was all in good fun," said Tracey. "Some quick thinking on your feet too." She really had great affection for her stepdaughter. She too had come from what, when she had been a girl, was called a "broken" home — her father had gone off with another woman, and her mother had secured a divorce, along with the harsh dip in family income that was inevitable in those days when women were trained for little else. She had backed Zed when he had sought to adopt Rose Sharon from her alcoholic mother. And she hadn't looked back since.

Zed's position became increasingly clearer. He reached for his cigarette, selected a Marlboro, and lit up, puffing a ring of smoke into the air. His wife regarded him for a moment, then turned away to see the Celtics slam-dunk their sixty-eighth basket on TV. It was the play-off season, and the Celts were battling for their lives with their California arch rivals, the Raiders. She could see Zed and Bob sit up and lean forward, their hearts pounding, her husband's much more so. Basketball was about the only thing that really got the men excited. The huge crowd in one of those West Coast astrodomes was eerily silent as the comparatively tiny crowd of Boston fans yelled and danced for joy. They were a mere two baskets ahead but ahead still.

"Classic!" cried Bobby, still elated at Larry Bird's twist — leaping right up to the net for the slam.

"Could be one," agreed his father, nodding. He knew the Raiders, with their many accomplished stars could make a comeback any minute, especially if Julius "Dr. J" Erving recovered quickly from his knee injury. There were still five minutes left. A commercial came on, one of those with a bevy of half-clad beauties by the beach surfing and sunning themselves, cavorting with a number of male "beachcombers." The advertisement catching attention and building to a climax — an anticlimax actually — when it turned out the product being marketed had little to do with bikinis or suntan lotions but chewing gum.

Zed once more returned to Rosie's prize, on whether the trip side of it made sense. Even at sixteen, wasn't she a little too young to be out there on her own? Of course, the arrangements seemed above reproach, for the American Embassy cultural exchange section would be taking care of things. But there was something that didn't square right with a young lady out there alone...

"But she won't be alone, Daddy," Bobby said quietly; he had been observing him and could read his mind well enough. He had learnt to do so by watching him each time he fell into one of those soliloquies of his during their many fishing trips to Vermont. By recalling the events of the past day or two, Bobby had always been able to pinpoint the cause of the withdrawal. Zed could even be this way while some fair-sized fish was trapped on his line, and he would not budge: He was that intense, always had been.

"Yeah, yeah," he muttered now, "I've heard all that. It still doesn't sound right."

Rosie turned toward him. "I know what the problem is," she said. "You really don't trust women to really look after themselves."

"Tell him, Rosie," agreed her aunt, "sexism is outdated."

"Well, well," Uncle Zed said hastily, "no offense there. I still don't think you —"

"Uncle," said Rosie, as she rose. "I want to go very much. I will be all right, promise. It's a chance to see the world, uncle. " She came to him and kissed him on the cheek and ran upstairs to grab her bag and then down.

"Where are you going?" asked Bobby. "It's only nine o' clock?"

"To make a call. Vince's waiting." Bobby knew they could hardly wait for the opening of *Tangling with Tarzan*. Though he and Vince were on the school team together and were friends, he didn't quite know what Rosie found in him. She was absolutely crazy about that Tarzan freak who went all over the place with a bandana and a spear, whooping and aah-aahing like the Ape-Man. They had seen all the Tarzan movies, read all the novels, both those by Edgar Rice Borroughs and by his imitators. But Vince often behaved as if he lived in Tarzan's jungle or some such place. He would go all over town looking for reruns of old Tarzan movies. And though she wasn't one to talk of it often, Rosie seemed to enjoy them tremendously. Women, thought Bobby to himself, you never know what they would do once they fell in love. One more thing. What did Vince think about her trip? She would be away for a whole month! Bobby bit his lips at the implausible thought of a lonely Vince; there was always some other girl. He made up his mind to watch him closely.

Zed and Tracey continued to follow the rest of the news.

-III-

A few weeks later and August finally arrived. The JFK International Airport was enveloped in a mild fog — signs of the gathering dusk hung in the far horizon, the clear blue-white skies with the weak sun opening up like a huge bowl of polished chrome.

Rosie Sharon Baxter arrived at the counter behind which blazoned the soon-to-be familiar name, Nigeria Airways. Behind came her cousin Bobby. It was bedlam. Crowds milled at one end of the checking hall; several dozen more stood inside the roped lines, their burgeoning luggage about and in front of them. Scores of relatives and well-wishers crowded the place. Ticket officials, sullen and exhausted, watched in trepidation as more arrived. In the midst of it all, a babel of tongues — from English to Igbo and Yoruba to Hausa and Efik and Edo — emanated from joking faces despite the anxiety. It was two already, and flight number 607 would start boarding at four, take off at five, and arrive in Lagos at six in the morning, Nigerian time, twelve midnight in New York. Ten to twelve hours flying time, nonstop.

Uncle Zed and Tracey arrived by taxi half an hour later to find them still in line. The younger people had left an hour earlier to get things going while their parents took in a bit of New York. They had barely apprised themselves of the circumstances of the place when the prize originator, Dr. Ebo Maduka, walked up. With him was an American cultural affairs officer; she would be in the plane and generally in charge of Rosie's month in Nigeria.

"Meet Meg Danielson," said Maduka.

She was a tall, well-groomed diplomatic type, about forty-five, no glasses and all courtesy. She shook hands all around.

"Great idea this prize," she beamed.

"Congratulations Roseline," she nodded at her, misstating her name.

"Rose Sharon," corrected her uncle with a frown

"Rosie to my friends," asserted the young woman with a smile.

"Then Rosie it will be," smiled Danielson. "Fits like a glove." Presently an airport valet came up to tell her her bags had been checked in on Pan Am International. She tipped him, and the man scampered off in search of more.

Uncle Zed unfolded his hands and took his wife's hand from around his waist. "Why is your stuff going by Pan Am and Rosie's by the local line?" There was an unmistakable accusation in his voice.

"Because it's part of the conditions of the prize," said Dr. Maduka. He had begun to get the feeling Mr. Zed Hubbard was not exactly thrilled by his niece's success nor sold on the whole thing about intercultural contact. Indeed, he had begun to see more than just a cautious uncle.

"The question is for Miss Danielson, if you don't mind," he answered sharply.

"But the doctor is correct," answered Danielson.

"Still that doesn't explain your use of two airlines," continued the irate uncle.

"You are right," nodded Danielson. "But I am not sure I understand why that makes you so angry. The reason is simple actually. I have been entrusted with a diplomatic material of some security concern. Pan Am is the only line flying into West Africa that the insurance companies will accept. That's one reason." The cultural officer turned to survey the slowly moving line and the marketlike hive and buzz of the place, then to Maduka. "The other reason, if the truth be told, sir, is that there are concerns about the luggage safety record of your country's airline."

Maduka nodded. "I heard it's a widespread concern in the airline industry generally." He lit his pipe as he spoke. "But I also hear they have one of the best flying records."

Uncle Zed, not listening to the last part, had already taken a step back. "I thought there was more to it," he said heatedly, causing a few heads to turn momentarily to stare at him. Not a few people had been read of in the press as going off their rocker at airports and whipping out some weapon or other. But only Zed's little finger wagged this time, his son tepidly holding on to him, his wife flustered in embarrassment, Rosie decidedly upset. "Then tell me this, the two of you. Tell me how Rosie's safety would be guaranteed in them jungles out there when —"

Meg's laughter broke through the tension. "Let us handle that, sir. We've been out there for decades. Do give the State Department the benefit of your doubts, would you? We know —"

"Yeah, like you did in Vietnam," mocked the burly construction supervisor. Wagging his long finger this time, he yelled, "Just don't let anything harm that child."

"Uncle Zed!" screamed Rosie, stamping her foot, "I am not a child anymore — stop treating me like one!"

"I am sorry, dear," said her uncle patting her shoulder as his wife dragged him away toward the door. "Be on your guard against the animals, man and beast."

Maduka blurted out, "I'd appreciate if you stop those racist remarks Mr Hubbard." But Zed stalked off without another word.

Bobby apologized for the family. "Please don't mind my dad,

he's simply concerned for Rosie."

"But I don't understand," said Ebo Maduka, puffing exasperatedly at his pipe. "Didn't he see details of the planned program? Everything has been worked out in to the last minute. Does he really know what the city of Lagos is like?" But even as he said that, Maduka had to catch himself. Having been out all these years, with his homeland getting to be more of a memory than a daily presence, what did he himself know about the place these days?

-IV-

It was the chilly cool of the early morning that really surprised her — aside from her great relief from the smooth flight, though despite its not particularly qualitative attendance. The first thing that struck her was the eerie feeling of being in a totally different world. Actually, it had begun in the skies — something like six hours outside of New York: The air in the plane had suddenly become a bit warmer, as if a giant's breath had wafted across the air-conditioning.

Rosie had been too excited to sleep a wink. She had sat next to Meg, as the consular official preferred to be called. It was a large aircraft, two rows of seats on either end and four in the middle. Most of the passengers were African, as was the entire crew. They were practically the only whites, with a few dark-skinned South European or Middle East types sitting somewhere behind them. She could still feel the unease that gripped her when she kissed Uncle Zed goodbye, hugged her auntie and Bobby, and walked off with Meg. They had gone through the metal detectors like everyone else. She had turned for a last wave; even from that far she could still see the lines of worry over Uncle Zed's face. Dr. Maduka waved and puffed at his pipe like a train engine's heave-ho. Then she turned, and in a moment she and Meg were beyond the security check-in desk and on to the tunnel-like passageway leading into the plane.

They had the window seats, she next to it. Meg proved at once to be a remarkably nice person — relaxed, chatty, and clearly concerned. "There is nothing to worry about, dear," she said reassuringly. "We will soon be in Lagos."

"What is Lagos like?"

Miss Danielson took a deep breath, then laughed. "Wonderful place — reminds you of New York without the skyscrapers."

"Lots of people?"

"Yes, lots," Meg said, nodding. " Traffic is awful. But the people are nice."

"How nice?" asked the young woman, her eyes narrowing.

"You seem worried."

"Oh, no, just curious."

"Nice, just nice. It's a different country, different culture. There are many things you'll find quite strange. Just keep an open mind. Think of it this way, dear. Any Nigerian youngster visiting the States will also have many more questions than answers."

"Really? Like what?"

Meg thought for a moment. "Oh, lots of things," she finally declared. "Like skin-tight jeans for one — how do you girls ever manage to get in and out of those? Like people publicly kissing at every street corner, like everyone in a hurry, the zillions of cars — all kinds of questions about things we take for granted."

The younger woman nodded. "I guess you're right."

"Well, what did you bring for entertainment? Any books, Rosie?" Meg opened her copy of Life.

In response, the girl reached into her handbag and fished out a copy of the book Vince had given her as present *Tarzan and the Wild Men of Anandae*. As she did so, a hostess's voice come on in the intercom: "Welcome on board to Nigeria Airways flight 607 New York to Lagos...." But she was not really listening. She was thinking of Vince. The movie had been postponed until a week after she was gone. She wondered if he would be going alone. Why, there was that Jennifer who often rolled her eyes at him....Would Vince still be there when she got back in four weeks? But he had given her the book, hadn't he? "Guess you'll be needing this," he had said as they sat at McMullin's, eating ice cream. He fished out the book from his oversize army jacket. "What for?" she had asked. "Watch out for the animals — hope they don't have you for lunch up on their tree pads." She had laughed and said thanks for caring so much. "No, I'm serious," said the lanky youth, looking out at the passing traffic. After a while, he added, "But nothing beats the movie, though." There was no disputing that.

-V-

The late model black Buick pulled alongside the airport passenger pick-up curb, and the doors flew open. The two women climbed into the back as the uniformed driver motioned a valet to bring their luggage to the back. As she stepped in, Rosie could see the caption, United States Information Services — Cultural Affairs Unit (USIS-CAU), embossed by the side.

The two men who had come out to greet them now stepped in. Meg whooped at the cool welcome of the air-conditioned air. The heat was beginning to get her, as it always did. It would take two days to get used to it all over again. To the flushed, reddening Rosie, it was like entering yet another world for the second time in twelve hours, a world that beckoned with a heat wave. Meg introduced the men: Jack Bramson, Senior Cultural Affairs officer; and the Nigerian next to the driver, Ben Odebe, a USIS official.

"He will be your Nigerian host," Meg explained. "His daughter is about the same age. She will also be a high school senior in the fall."

"How do you do, Rosie?" said Odebe.

"Fine and you?"

As the car drove off, the four chatted about the flight; the initial strangeness eased somewhat even as the first sign of jet-lag weakening made itself felt. Rosie would soon learn that Odebe had been a student in Minnesota back in the 1960s and had worked for an international merchant bank before joining the American organization. Like others in diplomatic and affiliated services, he spoke several languages — Igbo, Yoruba, Hausa, French, and English and had a smattering of Arabic as well as a working knowledge of some Asian language. He had majored in linguistics before his MBA in management.

They passed the airport gates and drove down the beautiful, tree-lined highway, interspersed with the tall electric pylons that ran across the city. The traffic thus far was light. A number of pedestrians were up and about. The early August sun was almost bursting through the skies, for despite the travellers' sense that it was already too much, Meg knew it was indeed relatively mild compared with the noon day highs yet to come. Nor was it long before they ran into the legendary Lagos traffic proper. For the fine highway inevitably turned toward the city, and the Buick joined the sea of vehicles and people on their way to Lagos Island; the airport was at Ikeja, miles away. The slow crawl began, with each bit of progress a carefully plotted move. It would take an hour plus to arrive at Victoria Island, the upscale quarters of the city where the USIS had its offices, close to where most of the officials lived. Everyone decided the two new arrivals were just too tired to see the USIS director at this time. So they drove on to Odebe's.

"Guess what I am going to do now?" Meg nudged Rosie. The girl stared at her. "Pass out for the day. I advise you to do the same. But first I'll see you are comfortably settled, that you have my phone number, and that you have a brief word with the USIS director. You will get to meet Ebere later in the day."

"Who's Ebere?"

"My daughter," beamed Odebe. "She is in school now."

"Goes to Queen's College," offered Bramson who hadn't spoken much. "Kind of like a posh all-girl high."

"All-girl?" Rosie's surprise was real. "Kind of like a convent?"

Odebe laughed heartily. "Of course not, of course not! Only that the boys are kept arm's length, which is where they belong."

- VI -

Rosie woke to the noise of strange sounds, with a jerk, forgetting in a flash the heavily-laden dream in which she had been flying under water, the sharks turning into clouds, and a million tiny fishes appearing like raindrops emptying from ceaseless thunderclaps. Now, as she rubbed her eyes and quickly looked around her, she was even more clearly aware of the room and the noise coming from beyond the closed door.

It was a pretty, airy little bedroom, the large, curtained glass frame windows even half-open. That way, daylight still came in while the curtains screened the harsh rays of the sun. A red flowered linoleum carpet covered the floor. A writing table stood beside the wall; a swirling fan atop it explained the welcome coolness of the place. A small round table with plastic flowers in a glass bottle stood at the center. At the foot of the bed, a yard away, was a wooden clothes stand with empty hangers. On the wall, a picture of the host family and a calendar with pictures of exotically clad men.

She now remembered how things had gone after they had arrived at the fine Victoria Island house. Obviously tired and half-asleep, Meg had written out her address, contacted the Embassy, and handed the phone over to her.

"Welcome to another world, young lady," the gruff voice of Director Elliot Parker came through. He had a familiar New England accent. She would later learn he was from Maine.

"Thanks," replied Rosie.

"You will enjoy it, believe me. You must consider yourself a goodwill ambassador from the greatest country in the world. We are indebted to Dr. Maduka, who is a fine example of the new Nigerian community developing over there. Don't be bothered much by the heat — the sun is both harsh and soft in these parts, and if you know how to follow the rhythm, you will....Well, tell me, how was your flight?"

"Well, very well actually."

"And how were things back in the good US of A?"

"Couldn't be better."

"Well put, Rosie, well put," said the old man at the other end beaming and fully appreciating what he saw as the potential political savvy in the girl's response. "Of course, it is the greatest country in the world!"

"Yes, sir. But I was only talking of my family and my friends." Meg tilted her head and came alive, fixing a quizzical gaze at Rosie.

The Director thought through that for a moment. "Of course," he said, "of course, you are from. . er. . . where?"

"Boston."

"Ah," beamed the career diplomat once more. "There!" with greater emphasis. "I understand you need a rest. I should be seeing you later this evening."

Director Parker hung up. Meg decided against saying anything and instead patted Rosie's arm and explained the set-up. Rosie yawned; Meg and Odebe left as she crawled under the sheets. She could barely make out what Meg was saying about jet-lag being temporary — she was worn out. Her eyes closed in what virtually amounted to an instant; the dreams did not take long in coming either.

When, hours later she woke up, she instinctively reached out for her table lamp. Then she realized she was not in her bedroom back in Boston. She sat up instantly; it was still daylight outside.

Rosie lay back on the bed and thought of Vince. How disappointed he was over the cancelled movie. He had been all rearing to go see it, given all the advance publicity and hoopla. Though she thought the Tarzan movies rather silly entertainment, she enjoyed how Vince and the others seemed to derive so much fun imitating the natives.

Finally getting up, she strode to the window, patted the curtains and looked out. She could see the cars going through what appeared to be a frankly broad street. But she was more taken by the grassy, reasonably well-kept lawn with a flower hedge next to a sidewalk. Two cars sat in the driveway. A little girl rode her bicycle about even as she spoke in a raised voice to a friend in the next house. The houses, too, Rosie noticed, all looked alike. Invariably two-storied single-family houses with the family rooms upstairs, the living room down, with a guest room, appeared to be pretty standard around here. A garage and a backyard, often with a tree, completed the highlights.

Rosie was unsure whether she should walk into the next room and meet her hosts — obviously everyone would be there by now.

She looked at her watch — she had been told to add six hours but hadn't had time to change things. It was 1 p.m., Boston time, so it would be 7 p.m. now. As if in sudden realization, her stomach ached with hunger. She knew she still had to take her bath.

She stood there, looking at the family photograph. Ben Odebe she could recognize. He was dressed in flowing gown of a variety she had espied on the streets; his wife was in an even more fancy attire. The children — four of them — were in Western-style clothing. The older boy was dressed in a three-piece suit, his sister in a white dress, another boy and a little girl — maybe the one by the driveway — dressed in materials of the same cloth, he in a flowered shirt and she in an embroidered dress of the same material. Rosie's glance shifted to the almanac. It bore the caption, "Nigerian Leaders of Thought." The pictures of chieftains, politicians, and others, who looked baronial enough, seemed all the same: puffed-up cheeks, gliding eyes, bulbous attires, bearing the unmistakable aura of their wealth.

A knock at the door made her turn sharply. "Who is it?"

"Ebere," said a voice behind the door. "Can I come in?" Whoever it was spoke in a crisp English that startled Rosie a bit.

"Yes, do come in," she answered with some excitement.

A girl about her age and height strode through the door. She was a good looking and rather quick, judging from her gait. "I am glad you are up," she said, extending her hands. "Welcome to Nigeria."

"Thanks." The girls stood awkwardly for a moment, taking each other in, as if sizing up one another.

The other girl nodded. "My name is Ebere."

Rosie thought she was cute and was taken by Ebere's attire, a flowered cotton blouse and a wrapper artfully wound around the waist, such as she had begun to notice among some African Americans at home. "I am Rosie. Rose Sharon Baxter. Everyone calls me Rosie. Who are those people out there?"

"My parents and people from the Embassy," Ebere explained. "Would you want to meet them now?"

Rosie shook her head. "I'd like to take a shower first."

"Are you ready to do that now?"

"Yes."

"Come with me. The bathroom is ready."

"Thanks."

At the door Ebere turned. "Oh, I forgot, you had a phone call from America."

"Already?" Rosie's surprise was genuine. "Who was it?"

"Your uncle, I think."

She laughed. "Uncle Zed hovers over me like a mother hen," she said animatedly. "Did someone tell him I arrived safe, and my limbs are all in one piece?"

Ebere started, "My dad spoke with him," she informed Rosie, hoping that would be helpful.

When, an hour later, Rosie stepped into the living room, six people stood up. Meg Danielson and Ben Odebe she recognized at once. A woman dressed in a red version of Ebere's attire she correctly took to be her mother. And two white men, Americans obviously, judging from their large frames and toothy smiles. Meg stepped forward almost at once to introduce the USIS Director and the Deputy Ambassador.

- VI -

A week later and much else besides, was a whirlwind of activities: visits to the Oba's Palace and the Brazilian Quarters of Old

Eko. Then she went to a fishing village, to a play at the National Theater, and on a shopping trip to the central market known as Alaba. Once in a while she experienced the pangs of home-sickness, but everyone was nice to her. Yet, try as she might, she could not forget the row she had had with Vince the night she had gone to break the news of her prize to him. He had been all ready and waiting. It was thirty minutes to a showing of a 1940s Tarzan film at one of those small downtown movie houses Vince seemed to know so well, which often had runs of what they called the classics of the "Golden Age of American Cinema." But she hadn't really felt like going. They had become more of the same thing: a swinging ape-man and animals that could somehow understand him, he and the animals in alliance against poachers and other despoilers of nature's last paradise peopled by hapless natives. She would have preferred going to the Boston Commons, sitting by one of the pools, and watching the ducks float by as the sun set and dusk appeared. There were sure to have been a few friends around. That was what had started the whole thing. He had refused to speak to her for two days after that. Two whole days! Later, to make up, she had gone to see the movie alone and had gone again with him — she had to admit it was as thrilling as the rest, despite the repetitiousness of the plot.

One thing, though. How long ago was it that Tarzan walked these parts? The Africa of steel and concrete, of hustle and bustle — how such so different from the jungles and vines and animals that was the stuff of the movies. Of course it must have been sometime in the past — but could everything have been so different in a mere thirty, forty or so years? She didn't know the answer to that. But certainly it must have been exciting in those days! She wondered whether Tarzan roamed these parts or somewhere else; she knew Africa was vast and had over four dozen countries.... Yes, she missed

Vince. She wondered what he would be up to? He always looked handsome, tall and gangly as he was, always moving with a breathless pace, so much fun to be with even as he gave his Tarzan whoops at every little opportunity.

"See," cried Ebere, "that's the Atlantic!"

"The Atlantic?"

"Yes, the same as goes up to America."

"Like the one near Boston?"

Ebere nodded. "Same water. That was how come it was easy to carry off all those slaves in those days — from one end to the other."

"Interesting," Rosie muttered, looking across the blue distance.

The popular Bar Beach was crowded with Saturday merrymakers. They had come with Meg Danielson and Ebere's mother. The two older women sat on beach chairs underneath a huge umbrella, looking out at the waves and the beachcombers, sipping soft drinks, chatting. The girls, in beach clothes, walked on the sands, across dozens of tourists.

Even for Meg it had been an event-filled week. Meg and a driver who acted as guide, had taken Rosie on a tour of the city: rather grand place with a lot of old buildings, hurrying people, and a little bit too crowded and dirty — just like New York City. She found herself wondering what Tarzan would have made of the traffic tie-ups and all that. Did he ever visit an African city?

She had also visited the schools, some nicer than others, especially Queens College — the high school she had heard so much of. She had lunch with Ebere and her friends and had watched the girls practice a type of basketball they called netball. She had wondered why they were in school this late in the summer. Ebere had said they were actually due to close in a few days.

Then she had entered the activities of the week in her diary, for she was to write an essay that might be published in the papers, if it were any good. And she had sent postcards to everyone at home too — Uncle Zed, Aunt Tracey and Bobby. To Vince, she had written a letter, actually signing it, "Love, Rosie."

That night the two girls sat in the living room after dinner. They planned to stay awake till eleven — a Tarzan movie would be on television. Rosie was truly astonished to learn Ebere knew so much about Tarzan of the Apes. They were in her room, and Ebere saw her gift from Vince. That was how they discovered they had even more in common. Then Ebere left the room, only to return with the large stacks of novels she and her brothers gobbled. All the Tarzans were there! But there were others too, mostly adventure stories — those that came in a series dominated. There were the many James Bond and Sherlock Holmes types — but especially the Tarzans.

With a laugh Rosie said, "One day I'd love to meet this Tarzan." Ebere burst out laughing at the joke.

-VII-

Rosie was the first to see the characters swing down from the trees, seemingly without effort. The girls filed singly behind the men in the far distance. A lone white girl, her pale skin glistening in the sun from the rays bouncing off the wetness from the stream, seemed more eager than the rest. They walked along the narrow pathway, ancient palm and ugba trees flanking them either side. The chief, Ojo Mahia, who also doubled as a high priest, was a medical doctor who had heard his people's call to serve as a guardian of the shrine of Tarzan and had left his practice in dutiful obedience to the honor. Rosie was not immediately sure of whether the large bronze-skinned European man in the leopard skin bikini pants and a quiver of

To Tangle with Tarzan 137

arrows slung across the shoulders, was the son of Tarzan — or Tarzan himself. But wouldn't the lost son of the House of Greystoke be very old now? And who were those others in the background looking like Hollywood filmmakers, packages, and Madison Avenue publicists? Oh, but there were animals alright — the lions, the elephants, the gorillas and the hippopotamuses, the Herons and the eagles. There were the evil Antmen too and all the other monsters and ghosts the great Edgar Rice Borroughs had written so much about.

Now the giant ape-man raised his glinting matchet and motioned the priest-chief and the maidens to follow him.

Rosie's heart leapt for joy. Now she knew her story would be something — Vince and Bobby would read about this, and Ed Wagner would interview her with more regard. There might even be talk-show appearances and all that. Rosie would find out what happened later, when it became clear she and Ebere were missing. It was not until Meg Danielson strode through the central partition into his office that Ebere's father knew anything was amiss; it was getting on to four and about time to leave for the day.

Meg Danielson's face was red, worried and not because she had just strode in from the steamy outside. "Have you heard from your girl today, Obe?"

Odebe yawned. "Why, no. Do you — ?"

Meg was businesslike. "Their escort has lost track of them."

Odebe sat up straight. "What does that — ?"

"It means," she snapped, "there could be trouble."

Odebe was already on his feet. "Why? — What — it doesn't really—" He reached for the phone.

Meg Danielson rattled off non-stop as the secretaries gathered to take instructions: "Call the ambassador at once — no press statements — no calls yet to the girl's family in Boston — but alert the police at once — assemble a crisis committee — been gone for ten hours, out of sight of their guides sounds bad — could be a kidnap case — with Middle East terrorists everywhere who could be sure Africa was not going to be the next theater? After all there had been that air hijack at Entebbe under Idi Amin...." With efficiency and purpose, Miss Danielson saw to it that every angle was covered. Finally, she placed a special call to the CIA station chief, who had notified the FBI back home. If by morning there was no good news, the crisis would be upgraded to full emergency, and everyone would swing into action — all over the world, or the girl may well have been spirited out of Nigeria.

The first shock for Meg came when she arrived at the Eleke Crescent offices of the United States Embassy. The press was already there, having responded with shameless alacrity, like blood hounds to the scent of blood. They were all there — BBC, AP, TASS, AFP, and UPI — mostly the foreign media that seemed to have their own leash on world communications. The local press might yet hear of this, maybe tomorrow, maybe not — but from the foreign wires, perhaps by way of London and New York, retransmitted to Lagos. She knew in the next half-hour the news of the missing or kidnapped girl would be all over the world.

One of the journalists who had once interviewed her on her cultural exchange program recognized her as she came hurrying up. Genuinely upset, Meg Danielson literally trotted off in the opposite direction, ducking through a tiny side entrance held open by one of the Marine guards.

****

Nearly everyone back home would remember where they were when the news of the missing girls came across the screen. Most apparently first heard it on *The CBS Evening News with Dan Rather* who had promised to announce it as a just-breaking news flash.

Uncle Zed had just come back from work and sat down to his usual dinner at half past six. He invariably took his time going through the three-course meal. Though he and Tracey had taken the doctor's warning on weight seriously enough, he was not one to forgo the pleasures of a life-time of good feeding unless there was compelling reason to do so. The three of them — Zed, Tracey, and Bobby — sat there at the table, watching the last few minutes of Archie Bunker and *All in The Family*. Archie, the lovable Queens, New York bigot, this time around got the last word on his outrageously liberal live-in son-in-law Michael by sticking out his tongue and giving him the evil eye at the same time. Then the perennial commercials. By the time it came to the seven o'clock news, Uncle Zed was just sitting back to take in a gulp of beer. Then came the announcement.

"Africa, Nigeria. American girl from Boston missing." Everything froze for a moment. Then the shattering glass. Ed Wagner's voice was steady as he gave further details — but it was all too brief. Bobby was the first to hop over to the tube — Zed and Tracey right behind him. "The details as known: Rose-Sharon Baxter had been reported missing by the American Embassy in Lagos. The young woman, who had left Boston seventeen days ago, was on some sort of travel program aimed at fostering international understanding of Africa. The report was that she had last been seen in the company of the daughter of her host, a USIS official and a group of wild-haired men who may be their abductors. Local authorities are afraid that young Miss Baxter is a kidnap victim of a group that may be involved in some sort of erotic ritual sacrifice."

Bobby's jaw dropped, Tracey crossed herself in the Italian fashion, and Uncle Zed sank with his full weight onto the nearest sofa, barely making it. Zed turned to glare at his family as if to say see — didn't I tell you?

The good doctor, Maduka, in his turn, had just finished looking at the textbook in his office at Boston University. It was a new interpretation of general economics from a socio-cultural perspective. He was wondering if that wouldn't fit his approach to teaching economics "as if people mattered" in the phrasing of a scholarly dissenter, who never tired of denouncing his discipline's seeming escape into dizzying mathematical heights and elegant forecasts, which often proved to be no more reliable than old-fashioned logical deductions. He sat back in his tiny office to do what he often did at this time of day, put his legs up, smoke his pipe, and contemplate his world. After all, it was six o'clock and the end of the working day for all reasonable men with no vaunting ambition.

His family invariably dominated his thoughts. Barbara, his American wife, hadn't called him in a month; it was obvious the Canada cult had gotten complete control. It was also clearer he must obtain a divorce and make some kind of arrangement for Mike and Sherene. He always found it unpleasant thinking about what he considered one of life's cul-de-sacs, for which his colleagues thought him silly for mooning over so much. It was clear his marriage was over, and he needed to deal with it as such.

The phone rang. It was from Washington, the State Department. What he heard in the next few moments made him straighten up. It was even more astonishing when he raced home and threw open his door, only to see three men stand up from his sofa. The FBI could always be quick when the occasion demanded. They had tracked his movement and his phone conversation the moment the story reached the embassy in Lagos.

****

As for those back in Boston, when Ed Wagner and Vince and old Mr. Danzig and Rosie's classmates heard the awful story, they were stunned beyond words. Vince for one vowed not to eat until she was found, creating enough sensation to have a posse of pressmen camp outside his home on Brattle Street.

Uncle Zed's reaction was virtually predictable. He had gone outside after that killing glare at Tracey. He tried to look up at the skies, but couldn't. The dying sun blinded him even as the heat seemed to sear his massive body. He didn't want to look down on the street below with its dizzying mix of people and cars in motion.

He went back into the hotel room. It was a modest but neat affair: a bed covered with a white sheet and red blanket, a fan, a wooden desk and chair and a radio on the desk. He sank onto the bed, having put on the fan. As he fought sleep, he thought of what a long week it had been, of how the world was indeed, as they say, such a truly small place: one moment in Boston, next in Alabama, then in New York, and now here, thousands of miles nowhere, in the heart of Africa. He had only heard of Nigeria, of Lagos, from Rosie, after she won that damned prize.

Zed had left JFK half a day earlier. It had been an unusually cold day, the same as when they had come to see Rosie off. To his wife's and daughter's tearful entreaties that he leave things up to the authorities and hope for the best, he had assured them he would do nothing stupid. So far he had kept his word. He had been quiet and pensive in the plane — a Pan Am carrier filled to his surprise with American businessmen and assorted travellers. They had made a stop at Monrovia where half had gotten off. More Africans had come on board, and he had once more closed his eyes. After one more hour, the plane landed in Lagos.

Another hour later, following customs checks, clutching his

carry-on bag the while — he had brought only a pair of trousers and a couple of shirts and a tie that should be crumpled by now — he had walked through a sea of human faces. He had long believed that most major American airports, from Logan to Kennedy to O'Hare, were dangerously crowded. Lagos beat the odds, if only because somehow everyone found their way through the bee-hive. Beset with nervousness he did his best to conceal, he could only see a handful of whites here and there, some red and swarthy in the heat, most obviously long in the tropics. But he had no trouble finding a taxi — or, what was more accurate, being propelled to one — as half a dozen drivers, acting as their own hagglers, accosted him in the most accented English he had ever heard, making that damned professor who awarded the damned prize, seem more American than he could have imagined possible. And they knew precisely where the USIS and the Embassy were located. All through the two hours of a meandering traffic that immediately struck him as monstrous, his mind focused once more on his niece, on his family, on his game plan. Still he could not but take in a bit of the atmosphere: The city could have been something out of medieval history, so strange he could almost be placed back in time. Flashy highways appeared to nestle among a group of endlessly grey, aged houses. People, more people everywhere, on occasion, at what appeared to be a bus stops, milled and massed in enough strength and confusion as to remind him of the despicable streets of downtown New York. Cars seemed to whizz past at a frantic pace on the expressways only to get bogged down with infuriating slowness in some winding streets. He had also seen the box-back lorries with people and things hanging by the sides in seeming stoic abandon. He would hear later that macabre humorists referred to those lorries as mobile coffins... His friends had briefed him fairly well on what they had heard of the capital city of Africa's most populous and wealthiest land.

****

Hours later, Zed lay still on the bed, half reflecting, half mapping out a strategy of where to begin the search. Meg Danielson, that stiff-necked spinster at USIS, trying to manipulate him. She had indicated someone would be stopping by at the hotel later; he must remember to let them know his presence was mum. He would handle this thing his own way.

He recalled the astonishment with which Meg had received him.

"You!" she gasped, more than cried. "I just spoke to your wife, who said she hadn't seen or -"

"And so she hadn't," snapped Zed. "That's not important. What matters is that I'm here to take my little girl home. You better tell me what—"

"Now, now," said Meg Danielson, calming herself. "Have a seat. You haven't even asked me what happened."

"Unless the *New York Times* is lying in its reports, all that I care to hear, I have," he bellowed. "If you expected me to sit on my behind and do nothing, you don't know me."

"Of course not, of course not," Meg said, nodding. "This whole thing has been a total shock for me too. For over fifteen years we've had people come and go on this sort of exchange program without incident."

She went on talking, trying to explain. Zed was hardly in the mood to listen. Dropping his bag on the chair, he paced the office, ignoring its familiar American decor — the large polished table with a small American flag implanted amongst a sheaf of documents and things, the two easy chairs for visitors, the three medium-high shelves on the left wall with a number of heavy volumes, the maps of the U. S. , Nigeria, and the world on the right wall; and next to Meg's seat, the lightly curtained glass window, looking out onto a great broad road about which the traffic actually seemed to move in even more bewildering disarray. He was still in a half-suppressed rage. But only one thing concerned him: How could something so dumb have been allowed to happen? Surely the Nigerian employee must be well known to the USIS? Surely Meg Danielson should have known better than to trust a potential terrorist?

"No, no, Mr. Hubbard," said Meg gravely. "I wouldn't call the man we know a potential —"

"It's obvious you guys out here are too trusting," snapped Zed with undisguised contempt.

The secretary came in with a pot of coffee. Zed declined — unless they had tea. She went to get some. Meg poured herself a cup. The phone rang. A German newsman just breezing into Lagos wanted to have an update, generally to know all there was to know; she referred him to Information. "It's been like this over the last ten days — the jetsam and flotsam of the world media circling in." Zed winced.

Meg Danielson apologized. "I didn't mean that in a literal sense."

"I really don't care in what sense." He wiped his brow. "Have you noticed it's steaming in here?"

"But the air-conditioning is on."

"I don't feel anything."

Meg hurried across to raise the knob a few notches. The entrance of the secretary with tea saved the moment. It was clear to Meg that under the circumstances two things ought to be considered urgent: taking extreme care with this agitated man, and getting him a hotel room. It was high noon, but obviously Zed needed a rest. She reached for the phone to do a number of things: to ask the secretary to see where a room could be found, to inform her superiors of the arrival of the missing girl's guardian, and to get an update from the police on their latest effort. Just then the phone rang. It was the Boston TV man, Ed Wagner. "No new developments, Mr. Wagner." Again she noticed her visitor start.

****

The son of Tarzan led the visitors to the village of Tarzwood — and there the real excitement began. There were scores and hundreds of ape-men romping around in what one of them immediately told Rosie was their favorite dance, the Hollywood Tarzan Shuffle, the Tarzwood Shuffle as the world would come to know it once the craze caught on in the discotheques of New York and beyond, often to be confused with the boogie-woogie fad that came and went every so often.

The girls and the good priest-chieftain stood with the leader of the large bronze-skinned progeny of the Legend. They danced in sets of five, sweeping across in effusive welcome. It was incredible how with one leap all five could spring off the ground onto the tree vines and twines and do a mid-air somersault, still landing on their feet all at the same time. Rosie had seen acrobats before; she had seen them when the Ringling Brothers Circus had come to the Boston Commons, but this was something else.

Then the animals stepped forward to do the Tarzwood Shuffle, as the Son of Tarzan informed them. After this welcome, he further said, they would romp across Africa to see the old Jungle Lord himself. Tarzan of the Apes was still alive and well, resting somewhere in the caves of Zimbabwe dictating his memoirs to none other than the mighty Edgar Rice Borroughs himself!

Young Rosie Baxter tugged at the Son of Tarzan by the arm: he felt hard and glazed. She said, "You can't imagine how thrilled I am to be in your country, sir."

The Son of Tarzan turned, and for the first time Rosie saw he was so like the actor Murphy Moore. The man roared with laughter. Then he gave the world-famous Tarzan whoop. Just like Vince — Vince's Tarzan imitation was so real, Rosie felt. The Son of Tarzan placed a hand on her shoulder; it felt cold, despite the heat. "Works all the time! Works all the time! The set is for real, they think!" Still, laughing he moved away toward the others.

For the first time, the sleeper's eyes opened, then closed. Vince appeared and disappeared. Rosie turned on her side and went on sleeping. The room filled with the uneven snoring born of disturbed repose.

-VIII-

Rosie was awakened by Ebere's excited cries of "Rosie — surprise! Surprise!" Even then it took her a while to rouse from her deep slumber. She sat on the edge of her bed as Ebere repeated her message: She had visitors from America!

Rosie had little time to react as Uncle Zed and Aunt Tracey appeared at the door. "You alright, sweetheart?" queried Uncle Zed.

"Uncle Zed!" Rosie cried wearily, what with those adventures. But she also understood. "Don't tell me you came all the way to ask— ?"

Tracey laughed. "You know your uncle. When he didn't get your letter a week after the first one, that was it. He was sure you either had been lured into a trap in some lost corner of the world filled with animals and strange men, yes, yes, like in those old

Tarzan movies —"

"Oh, no!" cried Rosie.

"Or kidnapped by some wild-haired tribesmen bent on some crazy ritual or other."

"My God!"

"So to make sure, we took an early vacation. It was easy. We just went to one of those travel agents."

Ebere's curiosity had by now got the better of her. "What's this about, Rosie?"

"Oh, nothing, nothing," said Rosie finally standing up. "Just some home talk." There was an edge in her voice, and she avoided looking at her relatives. "Where are we supposed to be today?"

Meg Danielson, whom she hadn't noticed standing at the door, now spoke up, cheerfully; she had listened and chuckled to herself as Tracey's account resolved her puzzle over their sudden arrival. "Busy day ahead, young lady! The University of Lagos is having its own version of the open house — and since you may soon be heading for college, this may just be one to consider. They have very good programs in everything from medicine to mass communications. And you know, there are a lot of Boston-trained academics there, so you may run into people who have been on your street or even said hello to you at the Commons!" It was obvious Meg was enjoying this. "Well, we have arranged for you to join some of the women and their children for lunch at the Faculty Club. Later we will visit a couple of American firms in town. Ready in an hour?"

"Sure," said Rosie, obviously thrilled.

"There is even more ahead. Tomorrow we will take a local flight up north to Kaduna. Our protocol officer there has arranged an equally exciting schedule. You may get to meet one of the Emirs, if possible. Then we will fly down to the east where there's even more to see, including the oil city of Port Harcourt. Exciting, huh?"

"Yes," said Rosie Baxter, simply. Uncle Zed appeared a little dumb-founded, finding nothing to say.

A Song for the Parade

Benjamin Nanah

stood at the altar of St. Stephen's in downtown Brooklyn as the priest administered the marriage oath. Enosa, his bride, was the first to be asked if she truly meant to take him for a husband. She said yes, her eyes sparkling, the sacred hall and its one hundred witnesses seemingly held in suspense for a fleeting moment, for the ritual response, "I do." But what if...? What if she were to...? For — who knows in these strange times, she could actually say the opposite, throw off the white Fifth Avenue wedding gown and, hips swinging, walk off, as in the movies, dressed only in her jeans trousers and a mini-shirt. Oh, yes, sir, be astonished at nothing. So everyone held their breath.

"I do," came the soft voice of the slender woman, stepping from spinsterhood to spouse before the world. Relief all around. Nanah could hardly wait for the pastor to finish before affirming this was for better and worse. Within moments, it was over and done. The two-year preparation that had ranged from the halls of Hunter College, where both had met, to the dusky villages back home in Nigeria, where family elders had hammered out the terms of the marriage in nuances these two would-be New Yorkers might never fully understand. For them, it had been a whirlwind — from the courtship, the parties, and, yes, the spats to the bachelors' eve, getting the limousine, arriving at the church, wondering who would come, then getting to gasp at the packed hall, actually watching it all come to pass. Now, on to the reception.

Best man Oje Okolo was, as has been his nature, both participant and observer. He thought Ben and Enosa cut a rather striking figure — he in his tuxedo with the gold laces, waxed shoes and all; Enosa, her smile as enchanting as ever, even more radiant. Now twenty-eight, Ben knew she had become a little anxious as to where their five-year courtship was going, especially when he had been severely tempted by the Jamaican sales-woman who had, months earlier, come to sell them life insurance. Ben and Enosa had lived together for two years; in New York, that raised no eyebrows. The news, when it reached Nigeria, created a storm that hastened the pace of things. No one marries through the back door, the two cohabitants were curtly informed by her irate mother.

"Isn't it all so lovely?" whispered the chief bridesmaid, Anu Mamadu, as the bridal party strolled behind the bride and groom, preceeded by the six flower girls in their lovely pink dresses strewing the path with flower petals. She wished she could break into a song right now. Indeed, she had floated the idea of doing something different, insisting she could actually render a song at the moment the "I dos" were done with. Oje had laughed at the thought that she could sing, but he wasn't the scornful type; so she had given him a cassette of her singing for him to listen to in his car. Being a lawyer, she had assured him, did not preclude doing other interesting things. Oje always thought she meant to say: Being beautiful and sophisticated.... There was no question Anu was striking in her glossy dark skin, high forehead, and straight bearing.

But a song at the altar? No wonder most people thought her a little strange — an artist alright. The idea went nowhere; in these solemn affairs, everyone agreed, there were two sides to it — and dealing with God's portion was the pastor's to decide how. At the reception too, nothing amateurish. In a wicked moment or two, Oje had wondered if Anu really wasn't merely seeking to advertise herself, single as she was, wishing all this was for her, this gathering, all the smiles, the floating rice showers, the measured steps from the church to the waiting white limousine.

Oje Okolo and Anu Mamadu moved forward to hold open the door of the greatly elongated car. The driver, an Irish-Italian with strong, square jaws and a formal bearing borne of years of driving one of the Rockefellers, bowed as the bridal couple came up.

Ben adjusted his bride's gown as she reached out to give him a peck on the cheek; watching them, Oje knew that full-lipped kissing, which might be expected under the circumstance, was as yet an unfamiliar, seemingly unhealthy, new-fangled addiction. Africans would always feel uncomfortable with this, even at this center of the Western cosmos. Yea, a few things still survive this second transplantation. Bur for how long? "Thanks a lot, Oje," Ben said, interrupting one of the frequent musings of his friend, whose efforts had assured today's smooth turn of events. "The pleasure's all mine," Oje assured his friend as they both gave themselves a high five, in the distinctive tradition of their college days, with finger snaps. This always ended with wagging of the long finger, symbol of deep camaraderie. Now it was off to the Mathews Ballroom in downtown New York.

It was there, at the reception, as Oje would recall later, that the idea of the parade had come to him. He had watched, sitting at the high table next to the beaming bride and groom, as drinks and condiments were served by white-jacketed waiters. People chatted animatedly. And the music was on too. From time to time, as popular tunes swept many to their feet, the dancing space would be filled. It would soon be time to ask people to go for a helping from the steaming banquet table. Everything was there: Jollof rice and peppery goat stew, ground bean *moi moi* balls, fried plantain, *foofoo* and three assortments of soup to go with it. And much more — salads of various preparation and a long array of American-inspired edibles for Non-African guests who might find the pepper a bit much.

It was fully attended, as the saying goes. Entire families came — and it was suddenly clear a new generation, born this side of the Atlantic, was growing up fast. But the youngsters, he noticed, seemed a little lost. Many — and these were the ones not bored yet — instead sat through some of the highpoints of this cultural repast which each wedding had become these days. Neither the juju beats of Peter Obe, nor the *ikwokirikwo* of the Oriental Brothers, seemed to move them, not the oldest ones at least, to tap their feet. Not even the "*Afro-beat*" king, Fela Anikulakpo-Kuti, could rouse them. But Michael Jackson! The kids were on their feet in an instant. The Fat Boys, Run DMC and the rap artists! Why, they had even begun break-dancing with prize-winning gusto. Someone next to him called out to his son. Of course, they spoke in English. That reminded him of another fact of transplanted life: The old tongues were fated to die off. Most of the children would grow up speaking English. The older ones were clearly as American as apple pie. There was something definitely to think about, the larger picture.

Oje stood up and threw the folds of his *agbada* about him —

he had long shed the tuxedo in an adjoining dressing room, as had Ben and his bride. They looked even more gorgeous in the matchin light blue, embroidered *aso-oke* attire they now donned, he with his cap and she with her head-gear and red beaded necklace. Ambling amiably through the dancing guests, shaking proffered hands but unable to say a word that could be heard through the din of Nico Mbarga's ever-popular *Sweet Mother*, Oje sought out Asuquo Izema, a social psychologist at Fordham University. The professor, a man of medium height and wide girth, was known both for his good humor and incisive mind. That he had chosen to spend his entire career in the United States had often been a puzzle to the younger immigrants, most of whom, in contrast saw themselves as biding their time until things were resloved somewhat back home. But then their own children were growing, becoming teenagers, they themselves battling the tufts of grey hair that shot forth each month reminding them of the steady march into middle age, even as they reminded themselves each week it was only a matter of time.

"These are no longer Nigerians," the professor explained. "No matter what you do, the younger generation, born American, is likely to stay American. Put yourself in their shoes, Oje. Despite its many shortcomings, and even discounting the bogus claim of its being the mythical land of opportunity, in view of the misery it has inflicted on blacks and Indians, and on many poor whites too, there is little question that since the Civil Rights era at least, the States has indeed been the preeminent magnet for people from all corners of the world. Don't get me wrong — this is no paradise. We know better than that. But give me a better alternative, all things considered."

"In other words," observed Oje as he surveyed the hall once more, paying attention to the youngsters prancing about, laughing and fun, "they may never become fully Nigerian."

"Yep," nodded the professor, taking a sip of his champagne, "unless efforts are made to anchor them to their inheritance, they will simply drift into some amorphous mainstream. They will always belong to two worlds."

Oje, a veteran of these conversations, knew where it was all leading. Same story told and retold by the growing community of African exiles: the corrupt governments at home; the lack of genuine opportunity; the ethnic trap that rendered one first and foremost a symbol of his group of linguistic affiliation, considered an odd person should one dare take a neutral stand on anything of public concern. But increasingly, something else, some greater threat still was in the offing — the seemingly coordinated attacks abroad that were taking its toll on the many hard-working, though self-conscious Nigerians. In the white media, from the vantage point of the black community, they seemed to hear it said: Those Nigerians, smart alecs, like the Jamaicans and the Cubans before them, are too aggressive. For the Nigerians, irritated to no end, the toll was telling. Many winced each time any drug-running brouhaha involving their countrymen was mentioned. Most went into paroxysms of pained embarrassment when the banks seemed to single them out, "tribal marks" and all, as credit card scam artists. In speaking of the two hundred and fifty, many would complain, these holier-than-thous ignored the other two hundred and fifty thousand.

Nodding, Oje felt the outlines of a project take shape in his mind. In this land of first impressions, one's image is part of one's economic well-being. Everyone knew that. Who got loans and how much? That's what makes the difference between becoming an owner or remaining owned. Then someone would raise the point best expressed in the adage of the new chicken in the yard who must need stand on one foot and survey the lay of the land. Then again someone would bring up a Western adage that said "when in Rome do as the Romans do," which was what everyone was doing, both those who worked themselves to death and those who chose the short-cut to the end result that counted material success measured in bank notes. Oje had been in enough of this sort of back and forth debate at friends' houses. A Nigerian Achievers Day, yes! Oje turned to go, but Anu, the chief bridesmaid, was already waiting to lead him to the floor where Ben and Enosa had stepped out to join their guests for a lively owa mbe group dance. The best man must always shelter the excited but tired newlyweds, for this day would mark the second stage of life's three-step journey. The children must come, they must be raised, and only then would this life cycle for Ben and his bride, be done with. They would have fulfilled themselves.

****

The Man from D. C. put down his glass of champagne, wiped his face, and continued watching.

-II-

Two hours later, exhausted and well-fed, it was time for recollections and advice. The speeches flowed. Everyone, of course, had nice things to say about Ben — a great, bright, future in his palm. Enosa — beautiful, as indeed she was, calm, hard-working, future mother of many. The usual stuff. But Oje was still thinking. The problem with him, and he had known this to be true since his days as a student architect, once an idea seized control of his inner mind, the present tended to blur, even as he remained acutely aware of all around him. But this was important, it needed to be done. Something to say, yes. This is who we are — no matter what anyone else thought or might be thinking. Nigerian Achievers Day. It would call for an organizing committee and a lawyer or two. Endless meetings — dealing with those who would denouce the pretensious stupidity of it all. But the determination of a few would be triumphant. Then, the final day. The hall packed to capacity. The guests of honor arriving. Ambassador Hamza would arrive from Washington D. C. , his limousine studded with a visible, fluttering Nigerian green-white-green. The Nigerian permanent representative to the United Nations and the Consul General in New York; a number of other African excellencies and viceroys. From the American side, Jesse Jackson would be notified — but he might be too busy with the ceaseless demands of his Rainbow Coalition. From Atlanta, Andy Young, who with Joseph Garba, once Nigeria's foreign minister and later president of the U. N. General Assembly, had initiated an era of greater diplomatic contacts between Washington and Africa's wealthiest, if bedraggled, black nation. But General Garba had left; personal contacts in these things mattered some, he knew. Mayor Dinkins would be invited; he might chose to send his deputy, Bill Lynch. The Congressman from Upper Manhattan, Charles Rangel, might make an entrance as part of his weekend rounds to his constituency. Queen Mother Moore, bent and still vigorous in her nineties, she might be there as well. So would those Nigerians who had squeaked up the celebrity ladder in this strange land of possibilities and impediments: most notably, Olajuwon, the basketball star, and Innocent Okoye, the rising football titan. He wondered where the gifted singer Sade Adu had disappeared to. Might be possible to interest some of the Nigerian moguls with vast international connections, at home in Lagos as they were in London and New York: Arthur Nzeribe, M. K. O Abiola, Waziri Ibrahim, and many others. But for sure only those running for something or other in the Third Republic might show up — but that would be if the military barons were ever really to return power to the people. Were Pa Orlando Martins still alive today, his Hollywood past might have been thrown in as part of the solid long links since the Second World War. Someone might recall that the links were made even earlier, in the 1930s when Nnamdi Azikiwe had arranged for Kwame Nkrumah and the other Argonauts — Mbadiwe, Man of Timber and Caliber, and Mbonu "Boycott-all-Boycottables" Ojike, the cultural nationalist — to follow his path in search of the "Golden Fleece" to Lincoln University and then to Columbia. Around the semi-circular high table then, would be seated a great many interesting people. Sure.

Then there would be the honorees — a group of eleven: eight men and three women. The four-person selection panel would be seated at another table, their papers at the ready. Then would come the awards themselves, highlight of the evening. Someone from the committee would explain the ten categories — science and technology, business and management, the arts and literature, medicine, law, accounting, and other professions, the whole lot. He would go into some detail on the accomplishments of the twenty nominees in each area, how impossible it had been to select any clear winner, the several meetings of the committee. People would gasp at the number of Ivy League credentials, at how many had quietly risen through the slippery career ladders of giant corporations and universities, garnering recognition at each step. There would be talk of how this ought to silence those bank managers drafting memos on the few scam artist, tarring everyone else with the brush that ought to be reserved for the rag-tag drug peddlers the press has taken to dubbing "The Nigerian Connection." The image war needed to be declared lest the community die of image attrition.

Oh, but there would be more for that memorable evening. At some end of the hall, an all-Nigerian band, American-rooted — the

African Drum Machine, most likely. Their "Flycatcher" song had made the rounds at a few parties recently, with the makings of a hit. A back-up dee jay with a stereo jukebox would be present. Two videographers would stand ready amidst their cables and wide-eyed cameras. He, Oje, would, of course, be master of ceremonies. There would be preliminaries — prayers to the Christian and the Moslem God, libations to the ancestors and the Gods of Africa. The guests would have been introduced and seated. He would begin by tapping the mike to test it out, clear his voice, and announce: "And now, ladies and gentlemen, just for starters, the Igbara Dancing Girls! Give them a hand, please." And the drums would roll. A high-pitched song, in fast-tempo, arresting, would rise from the back, and the celebration of a new American presence, would have begun.

Ben nudged him in some excitement. Someone needed his attention outside. It turned out to be a deputation of Enosa's people come all the way from Nigeria — her uncle and her aunt, with a party of six who had gone to bring them from JFK. It was meant to be a surprise. Enosa's cousin from Alabama had seen to it. Arriving late, but still arriving, to give their beloved daughter away; that was important. Ben's clansmen, gathered at one end — their New York association's banner on the wall behind them — rose to give a standing ovation as the in-laws were ushered straight to the high table.

****

The Man from D. C. rose to leave, one more foreign guest among these new people. He was prepared for the meeting tomorrow. He had only come to check out a few things. He didn't know why the chief had asked him to handle the Nigerian official. Since New York was the center of their activities, it was logical to catch up with them here, listen to their talk, figure out some more....

-III-

Nigerian Achievers Day, New York, United States of America. The Man from D. C. watched in some amazement. He noticed the small number of white couples present, the rest being either wives or girlfriends of the Nigerians gathered here in their festive attires. Many had come dressed in assorted Nigerian fashions, eagerly gorging the food, faces beaming, glad to be living through a portion of a culture they had become part of.

The Man from D. C. , the FBI man, was long seated, readier this time. Whatever happened to the Diplomat he had spoken to three months earlier, during the summer, he wondered? Thought he was supposed to be here. Sent home in chains of some sort? Could be — happened to the best, happened to Columbus the Discoverer, didn't it? Stange lot, these. He recalled how worldly the ageing Nigerian diplomat had seemed. His long stories of how as a youth he had set out to help remake the world. He had come because his embassy had sent him over with a letter of protest over the singling out of their nationals in the media as crooks. The nerve to throw stones from glass towers, the African had intoned, crossing his legs. This diplomat was a rather bulky man, but he carried himself with ease. When would the West stop its blame-the-victim tactics? First there had been the slavers, he said, then the robber barons who teamed up with imperialist carpetbaggars to run the world. Now mankind had become hostage to five nuclear warlords, the awful nuclear genie having been first released to haunt us all, by the Germans and the Americans. A glass tower comprising all sorts — Wall Street stock manipulators and business partners of the Medelín cartel drug barons, financial dupes, wheelers and dealers always shamelessly casting the first stone at everyone else.

The Man from D. C. chuckled as he recalled his own riposte.

Talk of nerves, he had shot back, fishing out a cigarette. Talk of the kettle calling the pot black. (How the African had reacted to that one!) Who didn't know corruption had become an art form in Nigeria? Oil magnates with military friends stealing quotas for the underground market. Currency counterfeiters, import-export scams. Did he wish for him to produce the thick dossier from Drawer B in Basement Office C, on his country's networks, here and in Lagos, Enugu, Calabar, and Kano? Did he? Well, maybe there is something he must see. No one must forget this country is the only one doing everyone a favor by leading the fight against drugs. No, he had wheeled in a VCR and swiftly popped in a video tape, fast-forwarding to the section he described as "apocalypse tomorrow." A man and a woman seemed to melt into one in a surreal haze of smoke and nudity. It was a narrated production in which a male baritone drawl was speaking in the first person.

Out on the ground, in the open courtyard, the neighbors over and about us. Someone in uniform too. He is in a rage, but who wants to know? I see his cap with the eagle. He is a man, he's a policeman, I know, yes I know. Ha! Ha! Ha! Fire! Do I see everyone lighting up? Yes, everyone's lighting up — lighting up their grass, why some have pipes and powdery stuff to go with it. Indeed — who says civilization says freedom! Nothing more. You in your corner, I in mine, nothing in between. Bliss it is to be alive — on the other side of hell. I know. I was there.

The camera lingers — smoke oozing everywhere; bodies gyrating, then sinking to the floor. Merry abandon. Theme music. Fade. But no credits. The end. The Diplomat had turned to the Man from D.C. "You mean — this is real?" It was obvious he was shaken.

The portly FBI man shrugged. He looked quite a contrast to the courtly Diplomat: loosened tie, rumpled jacket, a cigar stuck between his teeth — he was obviously dying to light up. "Could happen anywhere. Your people here better watch it."

"But this is a worldwide crisis. Besides, those people are not Nigerians."

"Yea, maybe not — but you Africans better keep what you have now. It's all still simple at this stage, one more tropical paradise that ought to stay that way. Wait until you get your first batch of junkies. The disease will never leave. From carriers to users to addicts — that's how it all starts. I see your people on the move."

The Diplomat removed his horn-rimmed glasses and wiped them. "Exaggeration gets us nowhere. There will always be bad apples in any group of any size. It happens everywhere. Name me the exception."

The Man from the FBI stood up and walked over to the VCR. He pushed the rewind button. "One bad apple, sir, that's all it takes. One roach now, a hundred tomorrow. Keep'em down, sir, the first ones," he mumbled. "But the whole lot of ya boys here — and the girls too, they're into kooky things."

The Diplomat shrugged in his turn. "I'll pass this on to the government, I assure you. If this is the vision of tomorrow, then it's apocalypse." Here was a new war, though he wasn't sure for whose heart it was to be waged.

"You bet."

They stood for a moment in the room cut there at the Embassy briefing room, two middle-aged men. "We are on the same side." The two shook hands. The Man from the FBI returned the cassette to its case, retrieved his dark, worn bag, in which the diplomat imagined, there might be listening devices as well. The man put the cassette back in the bag.

The Diplomat was already at the door, about to leave, when

he remembered something. "Oh, I forgot to mention — you know there will be some sort of ceremony, some prizes, an award ceremony for deserving -"

The Man from D. C. interrupted, "You mean something called the Distinguished Nigerian Achievers Awards being put up by the organizers of something called the Nigerian Pride Organization? In New York, at Columbia University, on June 3rd?"

The Diplomat was stunned. "You know about -"

The Man from the FBI permitted himself a rare smile. "We know everything."

The Diplomat forgot to ask if anyone from the FBI would be there: It was important that they see the other side of the Nigerian community, the dozens of professionals and businessmen and gifted people, the ebullience and self-assurance, the silent majority helping build the economy, provide jobs, make investments, celebrate the best of this country.

That had been weeks ago. But there were other reasons he was here, the Man from D. C. When would the kingpins arrive? He knew these Africans moved in packs. Wherever there was some good time to be had, you were bound to find the whole lot. He had the mug shots. He had never been fooled by all this talk of achievement and all that. Smart chaps, these. But too many speeches and too much dancing yet. He paused at that: Maybe they have it right; work hard, enjoy well. "Isn't it all so nice?" a woman next to him said, making him jump. "Our heritage coming alive to us after all these years." She was African-American; he wondered what she actually meant. Well, so was he. She was no more African and no less American than he was. He turned away with a thin smile for her.

As people drifted home, most agreed that aside from the heart-throbbing dancing, the debut performance of Anu Mamadu was the real treat of the evening, aside from the unsung distinctions revealed of the award recipients. Tall and elegant in her flower-patterned robes, she had strode to the accompaniment of blaring trumpets and begun to sing the national anthem. The crowd, unsure whether to stand and hold their breath, had been mesmerized. Then she stopped, looked at the African Drum Machine bandleader, then at the audience. The Machine began to throb as Nigeria's latest musical gift to the world, Anu Mamadu, broke into "A Song for the Parade." The place exploded — aware that another Sade had just been launched on her career, if only she would stay with it.

It must have been about 2 a. m. The Man from D. C. was still waiting. The party was breaking up. A child whose mother was talking animatedly with another woman, came up to him. "What's your name?" He looked past the boy, noting, waiting. "Tell me! Tell me!" The child was in a playful mood. The FBI man pursed his lips and moved away. He still had to make sense of all this, these people with their seeming joie de vivre. The kingpins had to be here he knew. But his people had assured him about the kingpins. Were they Colombian? Jamaican? Indian? Pakistani? British? Israeli? Nigerian? Thai? Japanese Yakuza? Sicilian Mafiosi? Saudi? Russian? French? Brazilian? Irish? They would be here and he would know them from their table, their air, their gestures. Or he could dash into the bathroom and unfold the mug shots he had, pore over the forty-nine faces assigned to him. How do you tell a Nigerian from a Jamaican, a Jamaican from a Panamanian? The latter from an African-Argentine? "Tell me! Tell me!" The child had found him again.

Oje Okolo, a little tipsy and worn out, was beaming as he and the other organizers bade the guests goodbye. Anu Mamadu, now in a killer red dress, curvaceous, charming, joined them. She and Oje held hands as they made the rounds. (An announcement of sorts,

Enosa whispered to Ben, hatching a round of coaxing and nudging that would lead back, give it a year or two, to St. Stephen's, this time roles reversed.) This has been grand enough. A better idea for next year — the Nigerian Day Parade was as good as done. Up Fifth or Madison, Lexington or Third. The community was here; it might as well start living. Tonight, this was the beginning — if only for the sake of the children who needed to know. The end of the beginning, for the rest.

The High Dim's Revenge

Author's Note

This epic is but a vastly expanded version of one of a legion current across Africa and in many other lands. "The High Dim's Revenge" is thus one of several among the Igbo-speaking peoples for whom the encounter with the West — three hundred years after their first contact — remains as ambivalent as it has been for other non-Europeans. In the endless series of victories chalked up by the better-armed invaders, the cases of success inflicted with the aid of the gods, as at the Ogwugwu Dim in this case, or with matching firepower as at Adowa under Menelik the Great, or through guile and stratagem — as with the Zulus at Isandlwana — these have entered into folklore, if only as a reminder that there was something to be said for those old days, now dim memories in an Age of Electricity and a "Global Village" when the young look ahead with barely a glance backwards.

This epic is based on a story I heard as a boy of twelve about the first confrontation between the Ehime clan and the first Europeans to venture uninvited to the land — even as another conflagration, the Biafran war, raged death all around the huddled masses. Thus the real credit belongs to the grandees who — in the season of rain and thunder, of Soviet fighter planes and Egyptian bombers of the kworshiokor epidemic and the ra-ta-tat-tat of approaching machine gun fire — sought to recall halcyon days. This rendition of their more lyrical account is a salute to their determination that the past not die with them.

Consciously written in a contextual free-verse, I have provided an equally deliberately incomplete glossary of names, places, and terms that I consider might be helpful to a reader who wishes to probe further. Otherwise, the lines are supposed to convey a sense of the unfolding events in their own right.

I wish to thank the critic and professor of literature, Don Nwoga in Nsukka, who read the original draft over a decade ago. I also wish to thank the poet-philosopher, Ifeanyi Menkiti of Wellesley College, who urged me to get on with it!

Chudi Uwazurike,
Nsukka-Boston-New York, 1977 — 1989.

THE HIGH DIM'S REVENGE

-I-

Children of the Age,
Chakpii!
Whaarr!

Offsprings of the Magic Filament,
Chapkii!
Whaarr!

As you know, Little Delights,
There was once-upon-a-distant-time
When men were men
And women were women
And children were to be seen and not heard!

Yes, oh, yes, there was once-upon-a-time -
And once-upon-a-time is come again!

Chapkii!
Whaarr!

I now ask you -
You future of the Line -
How do you wish I begin this song,
This song whose tunes are hallowed for you
Song of this ancient soil, this land Nakanu
Nakanu that was of Akanu born

Akanu that came forth of Lolo
Lolo! Ah, Lolo, cohort to the High Dim
Dim Onyeka, Lord of the Buzzing Bees!
How do you wish I begin this song?

Listen then, saplings so young
Listen well to this song
Ponder even so the ways of the ancients
Ponder yet the ways of men
From things gone by learn
Of the flashing by of God's will
As of the glints of greed in men's hearts
Ah, yes, Little Delights, listen, ponder, but learn,
Always!

For the world has been on shifting sands ever affixed
Ever since the days of the Christian Eden
Long before the Queen of the Golden Ethiops
Set forth for Solomon's Jerusalem
Long before Caesar stood by the Nile
Long before Napoleon trailed the Romans
Agape before the sky-high pyramid of Gizah,
Long before the stones of the lost Zimbabwe.

-II-

In the beginning,
When all was nothing and nothing all,
Chukwu-n'eke, he created Ala, Earth Mother
And that bosom of her bounty that glows

When the Fire-Lord yawns his darts of rays
And which men came to call Nakanu,
Land of the Serene, Trap of the Over-Confident,
Chukwu to the High Dim did entrust.

Thus was Dim Onyeka
High Dim, Lord of the Buzzing Bees
Shaggy Dog of the Unchewable Ear-lobes
From of old bound to none
But Chukwu-bi-N'Elu!

And under the sway of High Dim,
Dim who blessed a man at his nadir,
Dim whose dread Bees paid sudden visit to the loudest
Not a voice of evil arose
The length and breath of the land!

Oh, yes, not a breath of Doubt
Nor of Question!
And destiny moved on its ordered course
From fathers to sons, sons to fathers of sons, pedigree eternal
In the endless cycle of coming and going
Incarnation to reincarnation and more
As the Creator had decreed of all living things
Yes, not a voice of Doubt, nor of Question!

-III-

And if Curious Ones
You wish to know what became

Of they that let crooked thoughts disturb their night's sleep
Go listen to the Ageless Owls
From the dawn of time at Ogwugwu Dim hooting
Go shake the ghosts
Of his priests gone:
They alone might know
They and no other!

Yet go not empty-handed, Curious One
No, go not alone, Doubting One
Go seek thee some famed Dibia
Endowed with anya muo
He will be thy Walking Stick, thy Seeing Eye
The famed Dibia will divine thy way clear
Oh, no, go not alone, friend, never!

Go not without asking
Go not without sniffing
Go not without slitting the throat of a she-goat
    turned he with age
And flinch not you must
As the frothy liquid squints forth
Flinch not
At the red drink of thirstless godheads
For its steam alone may pry ajar the granite walls
    of the nether worlds
No, go not empty-handed, Curious One,
Go not without asking!

-IV-

Yes, life was like that, ordered and more,
Like an arrow straight and set,
Its pulse measured in the comings and goings,
Ordained from pukeless time, infinity-bound.

The men they worked the farm by cock's crow
In song and in sweat, double-edged blades aswing
Their women beside them, double bent
Their grandees ahobbled, urging,
Their offsprings about
Gathering dry fire twigs, rooting the devil weed.

And each day
As the sun eager grew
Without fail fathers and sons
They would set forth on the hunt
They would beat the grass
They would shake the trees
Disgorge the earth, fire the veld
Spears and matchets and arrows at the ready
Fleet-footed after quadrupeds!

War — it was war of the stomach:
That other war of all against all
Was but to come, borne across the seas!

The night they would croon by the fires
A man and his brood

To roast yam and cocoyam
Done to be split in seven slices
Enough for all, each dipped in the red oil of the palm
The swaying palm, tree of tall fame
Life-Giver, Gift of Chukwu-n'Eke Himself
The Palm, hailed in song, present in legend
The oil they laced with the
salt from far-off Uburu
And from the brown waters of the
Mbamiri people
Salt which the long-distance tradesmen from Aro
Peddled the length and breath of Igbo.

They would sit by the fire
Roasting meat from the deep
Chewing fried breadfruit from the Ukwa tree
Scooping sliced ugba from that wonder bean tree
Drinking of the sweet wine of the raffia
When the heady sap of the Palm — always the Palm!
Tall tree of tell-tales
Was done with and downed in singing gulps.

-V-

By night the puny little ones, they gathered
To listen to tales of deeds past and hallowed
    deeds of valor, deeds of honor
To listen to legends of the grey forebears
Of how in the age of Nza-n'Oba
The earth had slit open

Yielding the first ancestors
Much like red warrior termites, fierce and driven,
And the world had begun!

Ah, puny little wags!
How they would hold their breath
As wily Tortoise ensnares the Food Drum
And becomes lord over loud Lion the Prancer
They would listen in awe and in wonder
To tales of how Ndi Igbo once had kings
Whose swagger led to their doom
Then as for all time: Igbo-ama-eze!
Was it for nothing that the Igbo
Say their middle name rings out:
    Igbo-ama-Eze,
They-whom-to-no-man-bow!
They-who-judge-all-born-equal
They who hold highest those raised high by the strength of their arm!
Igbo-ama-eze: the Igbo revere no kinglings!
Did you hear that, Little Delights?
If pressed they say it loud to the stars above:
Igbo-ama-Eze! Igbo-ama-Eze!

By night the puny little ones
They played oro, the moon all smiles
The lads they spun the okoso as the damsels dance-clapped the oga
They played hide-and-seek, search and destroy,
They played touch-and-die
Mirth and laughter for games of the deadly years to come!
And the puny little ones from Ofeokwe
How often they stole off to the Moon Dance

To join bloodless battles
With puny Little Others from Okpaziza
How on occasion Ofeokwe and Okpaziza
Would troop down in one body
To stand off the valiants of Eleke as the sun set,
Umuezala as the sun rose
Ah, Little Delights — was it for nothing that Nakanu
Was in those days hailed across the world
Single-Land-That-Felled-Two-In-One-Day?

-VI-

A time when women knew the order of things
A time before the coming of red nails
Of swaying hips and hill-high heels!
A time long before the craze of the wig
Before red lips and red nails and narrow waists, before women
Learnt to stand on those heels like Izaga the stilt masquerade!

Ah, yes — it was a time
When if you hailed a man Nwoke-Ebube-Dike
He invited you to palm wine
And if you called his wife Oyiri-di-ya,
She sang your praises to ebie dance steps!

A time now distant and dim, my Littlings,
A time when women danced at the Agbagwu
Their men aglow with pride!
Time when stout-chested valiants
       each fourth day headed to the Afo Mgba

To wrestle one another
Their hearts aswim in the sacred tunes of the Ekwe Mgba.

Children of the Electric Age, what spectacle!
He who wrestled with the dexterity of the male chimpanzee
They crowned Ozo-Di-Mgba
    They hailed him Azu-Eru-Ala
He-Whose-Back-Never-Bit-the-Dust!

-VII-

Do you hear my song good friends?
Those were times
When the man whose arm was strong
And whose head was right
Won fame far afield
From Nakanu, this land that glows
As the sun spreads wings of darts
To Eze-akpaka, those people of many streams
From Orie-Ndi-Agu to Afo-Ndi-Mgba.

Ah, what a time, little ones!
An age when the evil-doer
Was sent on the long trail
To the justice of Ibi N'Ukpabi
Ibi n'Ukpabi whom the Pink Ones came to call the Long Juju at Aro
Ah, what a time in trick or in battle
Men went for a spittle
After those men with feet all covered up
Toeless Wonders from across the seven seas.

-VIII-

You should have seen the world then, little one,
You would have seen the white-clad priests of Nri
Trudging past, silent, wise in the ways of the gods
You would have everywhere seen them too
Those locksmiths from Awka
Those keepers of the cave oracle whose name Agbala
Meant Deep-seeing one!

You would have seen the scions of Eri
And the wards of Agbala
Chance by those ubiquitous Aro
Whether up at Izuogu or at Uzuakoli
Whether up at the distant fastness of Nsukka
Or deep down the sea-going people of Mbamiri
Umu-Chukwu, those Aro blessed of Ibi N'Ukpabi
They had first right of passage, yes.
Not even the fleet-footed emissaries
Of dread Agwu of Umuneoha might dare!

-IX-

Umu Eri
Ndi Awka
Umu Chukwu
The runners of Umuneoha
All four most sacred of the twelve dozens clans
Though to be sure
Each time you were out and about

You still looked over your shoulder
Lest some Abam on the hunt
Trailed hard on your heels!

Thus the people lived, children of the bright lights
For Chukwuneke had so carved the earth mother
And made an order in the world for her offsprings
To the High Dim entrusting Nakanu
High Dim, Lord of peace Lord of war!
Ah, yes.

-X-

The day they came
    Those sun-soaked Pink Men
From across the seven seas
Many in the land sat resting
Beneath the ugba tree
    shy of the broiling heat
It was the season of little rain and minor famine
Season to make home of the farmlands
They had had a hard day
They had always had a hard day
The rest would do them good
Any rest would do them good
So these came
Toeless and pink and lost across seven seas
The Divine Lolo had said they would come
Since the days of the First Fathers
    Nakanu had known

But no man saw it would happen
    while he still had breath in him.

-XI-

They came
The Pink Men from across the seven seas
The fat book under the one arm
The long-winded metal pole beneath the other
The big black book they called Bible
The big open-hole-pole was the Maxim Gun!

The big black book
Brimmed with knowledge new and secure,
They swore
As for the hole-pole metal piece
We saw it knew but to spit fire
Yet mark you
This was new, this firecracker
Its flames not for the wife's chicken pot
Nor the steam nor the heat that warm the warrior's heart
When the drum chants summon the valiant
No, my people, no -
This was different:
Here is the swift flash
That sent a man home
Even before the beckon of the fathers!

-XII-

The visitors preached the heresy
    in their fat book;
With that firecracker they mowed down
    many a valiant of full length!
With that gun
They took from us
The voice to say that which we wished.

They sang their songs
And these were songs so strange
Extolling some one-god-on-high
The High Dim they denied his due
And they called on men
To turn from the Bee-God
Forever to bury the forebears.

Our ways they called ways that are dead
Theirs, they hailed the new life to come
And they said, Men of Nakanu,
New ways are better ways
Without plus without minus!

-XIII-

For long they sang, these wanderers
The land they scoured in search
All over they preached
To the Evil Forest they raised their banners

Still singing and preaching in pleas
As the land laughed them to scorn
As the valiants begged the Oji Ofo grandees
To let them make mincemeat of the heretics.

Ah, yes, my people: I would tell you this
    their answer did come
At first in trickles
    then in stream rushes
For they had the yam and they had the knife
The white man held the Maxim so he claimed the peace.

Too, there were those that listened
Many that scratched their bald palates
And stooped to stanch the flowing web of time
Yet what was to be said, what
To men that scoop bath-water in full-dress
Females that peer and see not and knew not they saw not!

But then, tell me, son of father
Do we mourn the exit of sickness
    from the homestead?
Offsprings of Nakanu
Lolo's pedigree
Was it not Lolo the farsighted
That bore Akanu
Then Akanu bore Nakanu
Akanu whose valor he breathed into Nakanu -
And from Nakanu we all came
And Nakanu's name meant hard-to-turn,

How come now men had so lost their head
    so lost count?

Ah, little ones
Here was chewing without biting
Here was blindness without compare
Betrayal without parallel.

-XIV-

And the land lay naked
At alien footsteps it moaned
Ah, what ubiquitous footsteps
Those pale ones and their dark acolytes
At their feet desecrated lay Nakanu
Nay, defecated, swore the wiseacres
What with songs of strange worship
Strange moon-old foods baked and fried
    and kept and not decaying.
Where is the freshness of the new-caught meat
Where the green taste of the edible leaf
Plucked off the yielding bushes?
Or their wears
Three pieces and four pieces
And the children sang all day
Toeless ones, Toeless, bare your sixtoes!

Oh, yes, Little Delights:
The wizened Oji Ofo elders

Though they sang not like the little ones
Yet their grey eyebrows stood on edge
As they watched heresy mount on heresy
Heresy that sought
To sweep the High Dim underneath the grey grass
Like some harmattan storm-dust
Might wash fallen leaves off the road!

-XV-

Come now, my good friends, dear friends
Tell me
Do we not ask
Before we eat
Lest we die
Before we are sick?

Do we not query the agarachaa
Who for years derided thought of family
And now grey and bent
Hankers to marry this day and next:
With whom have you been keeping the while?

My people
He that doubts the power
Of the boiling water pot
He that says all water is but flowing thing
Be it from the sky or the stream
Be it in storage or on the fire -
My people, he that doubts the boiling water pot

Should sting in his finger! He plays
With tongues of fire!

-XVI-

Acolyte!
Have you never heard
When the child
Has the knife and also holds the fire tongs
If the knife does not cut him
The fire yet might burn him?

Life is a lesson, and
The first lesson of life
Bids you count the teeth
    with the tongue
Not the fingers, nor with the far-off eye!

-XVII-

And now do I not hear you ask
The God-heads of Nakanu
What did they? What?
Ogwugwu. Agwuisi
Oparamba na Opara El'Igwe
Yes — Lolo Dim, and the High Dim Himself
What said they to the noisy ones?

Ah, yes: They looked
and they shook

They shook left and they shook right
Back and front
Grunting in the language of the gods -
In the voice men call guttural.

Ah, little ones
You should have heard the holy lords of Igbo
You should have heard
The pregnant silence of Ibi N'Ukpabi
Heard the crowing
Of the Cave-Gods of Umuneoha
Heard the rumbling foreboding
As Agbala stirred in the hills of iron-clad Awka
You might have heard the sands shaking,
    Children of Electricity,
Heard the earth rumbling from its deepest!
But only if you had ears that heard.
No — those godheads
They watched all the while,
Yes — they watched and they waited.

-XVIII-

And as one the soul of the land
Soared in supplication
In silence and in words
In song and in prayer as myriad voices rose as one
After the Isi Dim, whom we also called Eze Dim,
    keeper of the Grove
Scion of the first line in the land

Fearful Dim, he sang,
> Peace is gone, gone, gone!
> Lord of war — war is come, come, war is come!
> From across seven seas, all across,
> Even as thy bountiful Lolo did foretell.
>
> Dim of the eerie presence
> Dim of the buzzing laughter
> (And that buzz is no man-laugh!)
> I recall your battle cry
> Ring like three thousand bells in my ears!
> Nakanu recalls , recalls, recalls!
> Nakanu recalls how you bore its pedigree to battle
> How in dust-storms the two clans had fled
> And Nakanu had stood seven heads high!

-XVIX-

The Isi Dim rattles his Ngwu Egelege
His head straight and ramrod, he sang on:

> Yes, my lord, oh, yes my Lord:
> We are agreed
> The day the raw infant crawls forth forward
> To pinch the bottom of the graybeard,
> The graybeard will do well enough
> To crawl back forth and pinch the toddler's buttocks as well
> Ah, now — but who knows might have sent him?
> For only the evil child sprouts claws still on its knees!
> Who knows what might have sent him?

Dim of the ringing laughter!
You that buzz so loud and the hills twitch
From Aluwaku to Agbaja -
You buzz till the sandy plains
From Ofeokwe to Okpaziza stir in awe!

Dim! Life-sustainer!
You who gave drink to Nakanu
When he thirsted to death
You who to this day
Abide by that first drink
To feed Nakanu's scions!

Dim! Lord of all streams
Our water is muddied
Dim! Lord of the flowing waters
Our drink is sullied
Our blood is poisoned!

-XX-

Dim Onyeka
Agu Ogwugwu
Lion at the grove -
War at the doorsteps!
War at the gates!

Dim!
God that bears Nakanu aloft in battle

Sending all foe to flight!
Dim!
You that decreed the rites of manhood
You that cured the little one
Of his ogbanje
And smiled at the barren one
And made her fruitful
And she dedicated her firstborn
To the service of your will!
Dim!
Sacrilege by the path
War at the hearth
Where the embers dim cold!

-XXI-

Lord of war, war is come
Father of peace, peace is gone!
Here is kola, this, nut of eight lobes
Here is wine, whitest sap of the tallest palm
Here the steaming blood of the two-horned ram
Wetness for your seamless throat
Here too, the short-legged master of all tricks
Wizened Tortoise from the watery forests
Of the Mbamiri people

Here too, red-eyed white cockerel,
He has but pealed once
Here too, a full-fleshed mother hen
She has lain but a lone egg.

High Dim of the bees
All that is for you
Far from enough, we know, mighty wind of the forest
Only the little bow of the people
Only the hoarse cry of your people
Tell us, O Dim, what this is about!
Tell us, O Stinger, what wind is this

For it looks all so clear
This is war!
Father of war
War is upon us
Father of war
A silent war has come.

-XXII-

Ah, my young Delights — that Isi Dim Onyeka!
How each day he stood straight ramrod
And to Ogwugwu repaired
How he dug his Ngwu Egelege into earth
How he sang on and on!

> Listen, Listen, Listen, he chanted
> Listen,
> Bee-God of Nakanu
> Listen, Lord of Nakanu:
> Nothing is beyond you
> so our fathers before us witnessed
> So in our time we know.

Shimmering host of the thousand Bees
You glide surrounded by buzzing bees
    The size of sharp-tooth rats
You laugh and the world shivers
You are silent and the world still trembles.

Listen, High Dim —
Do we not say
The stone is shamed
The day the hen's egg
Cracks the nut of the swaying palms?

But come now —
Shall we no more see the rump
    of the proud cockerel
As our forbears bade us wait to see
Each time the wind rumbles by?
The wind has rumbled for many a moon
Yet the cockerel walks his way
His head high in the skies.

Father of war,
A silent war is upon us.

-XXIII-

The story-teller turns on his seat
He whistles a tune,
His legs tap a dance,

And he calls out:
Ah, Children of Electricity!
You future of the line!
Do you hear this song of mine
Hold me when I chant too quick
Hold me when I sing too loud
This tale of the ancients
Like raffia wine it goes to the head
This tale of men and gods
These deeds now no more than hallowed memory
Little ones, this tale calls its own tune

-XXIV-

So was it then, Children of the Bright Lights
One day the toeless wanderers from across the seven seas
The whole land did they summon —
They summoned Nakanu to gather
On pain of their Maxim boom-dooms.

They were first to come
The three-legged Ndi Oji Ofo
Ageless and wizened
They that led the land
So close they are to the fathers
One each from the twelve bloodlines.

Now they sat one end beneath the great teakwood tree
Each on his goatskin bag, on one side

Shining smooth walking sticks the children sang was the third leg
On the other side
The sacred ofo club
The ofo in which lay the soul of the bloodline,
   pedigree and scions all,
The ofo at whose thud-thud the gods stirred
The great ofo on which rested the life of Nakanu Omere-Dike!

They sat, Ndi Oji Ofo, lips, eyes pickled red
Behind them in seven rows deep
The lay of Nakanu, each man and his wives
Each woman and her offsprings
All tight-lipped awaiting the pink men
From across the seven seas
who had taken from us
The voice to say that which we wished.

-XXV-

Eze Dim Onyeka -
You ask: was he there too?
Ah! Ever high priest of the Bee God
There he stood ramrod erect and apart
Under no tree, under no shade
But full in the view of the sun and the heavens
That they too may witness this day.

See, see how he stands silent and erect
See, see the chalk marks all over him
See the white paint on his calves

the tall eagle feather in his hair
See, see the sharp-tipped Ngwu Egelege he grasps firm
The Ngwu Egelege the High Dim gave his forebears
Listen, hear how it jingles and dangles
    with the voice of a thousand godheads
    whenever he dips into earth and withdraws
His head straight and ramrod
He never once looked this way or that way!

-XXVI-

Ah, yes the land entire was there
A towering manhood assembled
The young men, chest out, tendons bristling!
See how fresh, our women
Even they that we brought home
Booty from Ezeakpaka, from Umuozu, from Obilo!
Why, have you never heard it asked in sing-songs:
    Come now, proud damsels, come now
    Tell us, speak up, come now —
    Are you of Nakanu born or bred?
    Loyal like the wives of those
    Worthy scions of the Bee God —
    So what then, this bragging?
Now, now: do you hear the pink one with the Bible
Say how wrong it was to keep women home
Hear them decree wives and mothers and daughters too
Must beat a path to the gathering at Afo Dim!

So then they came
We came — we all came
Side by side behind Ndi Oji Ofo
We all stood to speak of life — and of death
With women!
Do you hear that?
So who would look after the hearth?
Who would boil the water that we might drink?
So who would prepare the pasty porridge
Of yam and cocoyam for when the man comes singing home?
Who said the neck and the head are one and the same?

-XXVII-

So the land did wait
For the men from beyond the seven seas
Who asked us to desert the High Dim
To bury our ways

Well is all well:
The man who stands on his two legs
Does not begrudge to dance

Ah, yes:
Some day the wind will blow
And we shall see the dirt rump of the proud cockerel!

-XXVIII-

Then they appeared
They whose home stood seven seas off
And before the people
Did they raise him by the hand
Imp, the driven imp!

And he stood up,
His cheeks puffed
His eyes twinkling
He stood up, Ibenna, son of Nwiwu Taata
He stood smiling, waving.
Waving?
And on his head
They placed a blood cap —
On the red cap
They stuck their white feather
Feather from the lofty Eagle
Eagle, lord of the airy skies!

So!
All hail!
Warrant Chief?
Warrant Chief to warrant what?

-XXIX-

Ha ha ha — Dim of the Bees!
Hearest thou this, O Stinger so Sudden!

All this and silence?
Ah, Lolo, O Consort -
But Nakanu knows you notice!
Nakanu knows you know neither day nor night
High Dim of the Bees
Artful Lolo, Consort of the High Dim,
Nakanu well knows that which it knows.

Was it not you, Mother Lolo,
Who taught us of the hen's egg
Which when it cracks the nut
The stone but must hide for shame?

-XXX-

Warrant Chief to warrant whom?
Look me full in the face
Pink One from across the seven seas:
This land is called Nakanu
Nakanu of the Proud
Nakanu of the Free
Go ask the men of Ezeakpaka
Go ask the sons of Obillo
Go ask the wise ones of Umuozu!

No — do not look away,
Do not pretend pleading boredom
This truth remember you heard this day
It is but in the land
Where men have long breasts and round bottoms

The land where men wear earrings
And weave their hair like maidens
Flashy bangles on their hands, jigida about the waist —
Only in such land does Tricky Turtle
Pass for First Daughter!

Yes, yes, only in such land!

-XXXI-

Warrant Chief, O Chief warrant!
I now see why those twinkle-twinkle eyes!
For these ten and ten years gone
Have you not trailed the steps of the Toeless Visitors,
Sniffling dog for the huntsman by day
By noon carrying their Book of Magic
At night awaiting crumbs from the Master's Feast,
Tongue lolling, rogue eyes twinkling,
Greedy heart yearning for more!

We know now, O Chief Warrant,
You heard of the Pink One's Red Caps windfall
Red Caps here and there bestowed across and about the Niger
Steadfast your eyes affixed on it
On it over this land of the free
Nakanu that since time bowed to none
None of blood and flesh born
Nakanu of the free
Scions of a race that glides with the snail
And races with the fleet-footed fox

Content with the High Dim's Bounty
Direct endowed from the high heavens.

-XXXII-

Look me full in the face Chief Warrant
It is only in the land of those efulefu,
Enemies of ours, the lazy land of Obillo
The stiff-necked ones of Ezeakpaka and Umuozu
There, among them, Tricky Tortoise may dance
At their mothers' funeral and they would hail him First Son!

Look here and listen well!
Remove the wax that stuffs those ears shut
When the old hag insists
She must scale the yam barn
Do we tie her up in strings?
Ah, but no, never -
But we must hurry across
To gather her bones the other side
For who knows which godhead summons her?

Ha! The wind will hoot and howl
Blow till the red rump of the proud cockerel
Shall a secret be no more!

-XXXIII-

Little Ones, ah,
Innocent Ones of Neon Lights

You who would dance across the tips of the
brave wide new world
A world we but dreamt of afar
A world your forebears spoke of but in metaphors
This music grows apace
Like windfalls its roams the space!

One day indeed did the wind blow
It blew like a storm dust, like a tornado
It blew fierce like the combined blizzards of the Sahara wastes
And the gales of the Oshimiri water-sheets
Of the Mbamiri people
It blew once, ah, it drew final!
Listen, my dear friend,
There is some story yet in this song of Nakanu!

-XXXIV-

He led them
Warrant chief
Through winding pathways
Across virgin farmlands
And warm homesteads
Down to Dim Onyeka's hallowed abode
Ogwugwu Dim itself
Here where dwelt the Bee-God himself
Here chief warrant led
There, dear innocents, there he led!

-XXXV-

Now, what do we smell here, of
The little she-goat?
Did she not hear others were giving birth
And rushed forth one of her very own
A squashy-headed nanny, dead and shrivelled?

Listen, warrantsman,
Do not say it's the new wind of the world:
Nothing happens without nothing;
The stump that trips the knowing Tortoise
Is sown only by the knowing Nwadiala, son-of-the-soil.
Do you remove yourself
And say the hut is too small?
There is room yet.

-XXXVI-

They waded on ahead
Then they stood, and they stared
Before them a mighty expanse of tangled darkness
Ogwugwu Dim
Whose bowel never was clear
Save to the initiate
Nothing, nothing would they see clear
That sun-drenched day.

Yet:
Venture in we would
    - spoke the leader

another hawk-beak nose
To prospect for gold
To prospect for silver
That's why here we are
For I'm sure informed
There is gold here
And there is silver
Enough to make a Spaniard swoon!

Why, have we not over the world romped, my men?
From Calcutta of the Indies to Colchin China
From Buenos Aires to the Babary coasts
From Cairo to the Cape and right around
From the Cape to Kimberley, Kimberley to Jo'burg
In search of those metals mightier than all else!

For where gold goes goes everything else
Wealth and grandeur, aye, power over men and matter!
And I shall say this even as we are to strike our destiny now
Show me the man who is unmoved at the yellow glint of gold
Nor unstuck by the dazzle-rays of silver
And I shall turn back and set sail for Europe
Back to my job as a chimney-sweep!
Now my men — let's march in to the future!

Thus spoke the leader
And a roar came in response
To the gold and silver talk of the chief hawk-beak.

-XXXVII-

Ahead then they pressed
Seven steps they took, stepping on
Little lives that held their breath
Seven steps — and behind
Three clatter-coughs
And they spun in terror unconcealed —

Majestic before them
Head ramrod straight
Isi Dim Onyeka
Eyes blazing blood
His Ngwu Egelege quivering:
Behold the ears-and-voice of the godhead!

I warn you one and all, he cried
The mission upon which you embark
Shall wrought nil
But disaster
Disaster for you and you
One and all
His lips parted like in smile
And he broke into song
Song that was taunt
Taunt that was hint
Hint that was life
Hint that was death
He sang:

Pink Man from afar
Toeless wanderer
O pink and Toeless One!
He that may live a thousand years
Needs never be told twice
For God's wisdom comes in sixes
The Eye for ogling, sighting,
The hand for feeling, fighting
The ear for hearing, sounding,
The nose for smelling, sniffing, upturned
The tongue for testing, twisting
And the mind-but
Here the six go ayakata!
The mind where the six go ayakata!
O visitors from afar, where is
The sixth, the center of all wisdom

Stopping his song he spoke again:
He that may live thousand year
Needs never be told twice.

Hawk-beak Nose, he turned up his nosey face
    so full of disdain
That shaggy? That bogey?
Accost him, arrest him!
    - thundered he in order
And off his armed mess-men came
They went, went after the Eyes-and-Ears of the High Dim

Forlorn quest
For though they wove about him a ring
The Isi Dim Onyeka
Long had he gone on home and away on his way
Aloft carried in Dim's aura
Like the Bee-God used to carry Nakanu
In the days of endless war!

His message was done.

-XXXIX-

Warrant chieftain
The winds ablowing
The tornados acoming
The blinding sandstorm of the Sahara
The telltale storms of the sandy wastes acoming!

Ah, greatling!
   - what greatling!
Here he stood
Cringing
Torn between knowledge
And duty
The pink-brown one's duty
Between his dread of Hawk-Beak Nose
And knowledge of The Path

Petrified's the word
Imp full of ambition
Imp full of itch.

-XL-

So did they step on
A crew to behold
Lowered in steps so fateful
One after another into the sacred abode
The High Dim's hallowed abode
Here where no chicken strays!

What a crew!
A gang wielding matchets in song
Slashing holy grass
Armed with saws
To saw off sacred trees that bled blood
Picks to picket consecrated earth.

They carried shovels
They came with guns
They had too their dogs
Fat smooth snarling mongrels
They came
A small army
Led by warrant chief
Who feared half the time
It was his own warrant
That of he and his
He wore in that eagle feather!

-XLI-

Slowly they went
In habits so strange the birds smirked —
Ah, for the pale men
Their hats made of dressed-up pans
They wore khaki jackets full of pockets
They wore khaki shorts wide and airy
And down their toeless feet
They wore stockings and trappings
And boots that thudded the earth
Kpo! kpo! kpo!

As for our men
Bent with load so heavy
They wore no shoes
Still they were dressed in akwa-miri
And in two-arm singlets
All that made them no better.
For paltry droplets
Some had sold the patrimony.

-XLII-

But — do you follow my tale
Little scions of Nakanu?
Do you see, children of electric lights
How in steps into darkness, steps so insecure
Men without minds, yes, without sight
Breached the wedge of time and destroyed our world

The world that had come
Straight from Chukwuneke to the High Dim
From the Bee-God to the forebear Akanu
From Akanu and Nakanu and beyond?

-XLIII-

Thus did they descend
To where the water ran clear and wondrous
To where the sand spread either side
In the clear view
Of the most wondrous of nature
The crickets one across to the other
The birds singing merry
Quadrupeds full of love and fracas.

Thus did the digging begin
Hawk-Beak Nose
With his host
Had set foot in the sacred grove.

Ha, ha, these people
How they dig, heartily enough
Singing songs all day long
Their initial dread vanishing
In puffs of tobacco smoke
As picks and shovels
Disgorge open the holy Ogwugwu
Where dwelt the Bee-God Dim
Ah, the wound did bleed so sore!
The wound did bleed red.

-XLIV-

And Hawk-Beak Nose spoke in boast:
Unbelievers! Atheists! Heathens!
Superstitious crows! Savages!
Whoever on earth told them
The fullness of this bounteous valley
So full of silver, so full of gold
Could ever be the dwelling place
    of any godhead!
Oh, for pagans in their ignorance!
Oh, for peasants in their simpleton!

And Hawk-Beak Nose looked over his host
One after the other
And his mouth he opened
And thus again he spoke
Funny, Funny, isn't this all funny?
How the stupidity of the native
Sets back the march to civilization
How the savage in his ignorance
Holds wrong the clock of time!

And Hawk-Beak Nose began to guffaw
His men, too, began to guffaw
Warrant chief he too, did, guffaw with them
They all guffawed
Oh, how they guffawed
Till the sacred grove rang with their guffaw!
It was then the aura came

Gradually it descended
The tremulous aura of the High Dim.

The trees they shrieked
And Mother Earth rumbled
Anyanwu, Lord of the thousands sun rays,
His face in reverse he turned West he bent before the time,
Startling men and warning the third-eyed of the earth,
Sultry darkness at high noon
Dark clouds of portents without miss!

Ah, Dim of the Bees!
You come for the wrongdoer
But only when life is sweetest!

Ah, Dim of Nakanu — yes!
We weed about the little spicy ose mound
We do not climb it!
Ah — for the red rump of the wayward hen!

-XLVI-

Fast and swift they descended — yes;
From nowhere they swept in
Dread Bees of Dim
The size of rats
From the length and breath of Igbo they swept in:
The Bees of Dim that held the peace
But who in frenzy fly
When the godhead chose to stir!

You could hear them gurgle
In the voice men call guttural
The pantheon of gods and goddesses
Ibi N'Ukpabi in his long shrine safe at Aro
Agwu serene in his abode at Umuneoha
Agbala in repose at his oracular hollow
Up in distant Awka, that land of ironmongers —

And from the lean-lanky men to the north
The horse-eating warriors of the Nsukka plains
Down, down to the broad-chested Abam warriors
The much-travelled Aro
The fleet-footed Umuneoha
The fish-eating red caps at Onitsha
To the men of Igala, cousins twice removed
And the handsome gallants of the mbamiri clans
Around and about the word went:
Raise the right arm of strength
To the seafarers from afar
Raise it
To their nosey faces!

-XLVI-

And Warrant Chief was first that went
Down the gaping hole
Through some stair-flight unseen
Down down he slid
To the frown of his fathers

The tears of his mothers
The curse of the gods.

And Hawk-Beak Nose next did follow
On the ear-lobes dragged
His host following
Screaming, frightened
Propelled, dazed
And the rat-sized Bees of Dim
In frenzy buzzed and bit, dragging
They were sent.

-XLVIII-

Ah, my people, my little lights!
What do I say now my song is done?
How the red rump of the proud cockerel
Is laid bare for all eyes
    - profane and unprofane

The corpse lying in the sodden earth
Hails the flutesman: On, on tune flutterer,
The song comes through clear
Your song throbs the heart to tears
The music stirs the feet to dare -
But for this muddy hold
But for this sticky grip
It would all be something to behold!

But never forget yet, he went on

You walk first, off-spring of Nakanu -
Then you run,
Only then, only then!
Yes, you look before you dare
You went into Ogwugwu not alone
You sought the greatest Anya Muo
You slit the throat of a she-goat
    turned he with age
Before you confront the wonders of the
    God-on-High
Chukwuneke who in His wisdom
Had created Mother Earth
And that portion of her outlay that glows
When the Sun Lord Anyanwu spreads his wings of darts
And which men came to call Nakanu
    Surpriser of the Confident
Chukwu to the High Dim did entrust.

Dim Onyeka in Nakanu
Is never to trifled with.

-XLIX-

Now — up, up, wake up!
Children of the bright lights!
Scions of Nakanu, my little delights!
Ah, yes — it did came to pass
That fight of the past
It went on for moons on end
Other Hawk-Beak noses came and went

Their servants about the land
The armed power massed down at Umezala Erim
Their smiling preachers scurrying about
All of them in the meantime
Tearing our world a thousand ways.

But mark you, that routing at Ogwgwu
It but was the first, not the last
And many there who went the wrong way.

Give it to them then, I say
For this day
Only the Christian Lord
May tell who came to win
For the proud Dim, with his Lolo
On Nakanu their backs turned
For Nakanu had become full of Doubt and Question
And to the entreaty of the Isi Dim Onyeka
The high Dim has been silent
And would to none speak but in signs most vague.

As for those treasure-hunters
The deep bowels they dug
Do to this day remain
And will stare back at you
If you go stare at them

Be not deceived though
If you think
You may ever see

The spring hole
Leading to Dim's abode
For you will not
Only his priests know.

-L-

Yet if you may chance upon
The Isi Dim of this day
Descendant of that ramrod priest of the old
He may tell you
If his wife made him egusi soup
Sweet with bitter leaf
That somewhere deep down the watery beyond
There stand bound beneath Ogwugwu Dim
Men and animals pale and dark alike
Chained to pillars of bone
Daily whipped by giant bees
Their agony eternal
Remains to this day
A legend of the Nakanu
Told and retold by the rains and dark nights
Of Dim Onyeka's revenge
And the fate of Toeless Wanderers
Whom Lolo had foretold would come.

Children of Electricity,
Scions of the Day of the Magic Filaments,
Chakpii!
Whaar!

Who sleeps there — ah, awake, awake!
Chakpii!
Whaar!
Tales are proverbs and proverbs are born of the wisdom tooth!
The moon has gone to sleep
Ah, even the tortoise stares no longer
Man must to nature bow his head!

Now, Little Delights,
Our tale is done -

> *We thank you, O grandfather!*
> *We thank you, O wise one!*
> *We thank you most, O grandfather!*

Chakpii!
Whaar!

GLOSSARY OF SELECTED AFRICAN TERMS*

Agarachaa — aimless wanderer, akin to the "rolling stone that gathers no moss" metaphor in English.

Afo Mgba — the major market that meets on the Afo market day — the other days in the four-day week are Eke, Orie or Oye, and Nkwo — one of whose attractions is the *mgba* wrestling match.

Agbala — a powerful deity belonging to the Awka people, who were also famous as iron smiths.

Agbada — a flowing gown worn over a long shirt with matching pants, typical of West African peoples; (Yoruba).

---

* *Most of these terms are the Igbo expressions from* The High Dim's Revenge; *other terms are identified by their ethnic origin.*

Agbagwu — an Igbo harvest festival popular in the Okigwe area.

Agwu Umuneoha — another powerful deity belonging to the Umuneoha clan.

Akwa miri — towel, loin cloth in this sense

Ala or Ani — goddess of the Earth and of fertility.

Anya muo — literally, eye of the gods, one who possesses a separate eye that sees the world of the gods.

Anyanwu — Lord of the Sun; used interchangably to mean the Sun (Igbo).

Aso oke — a women's four-piece attire made from silk-ike fabric that became fashionable among the Lagos elite in the 1970s; (Yoruba).

Ayakata! — an expression that varies from cynical to laudatory, depending on its usage.

Azu-Eru-Ala — one whose back never touches the earth.

Bolekaja — a lorry-like bus typically found in Lagos, specialized in carrying market-women, low-income workers and assorted goods through the sprawling city; (Yoruba).

Chakpii! — traditional greeting by a story-teller at the start and ending of his or her tale. Often followed by *Whaar!*

Chukwu-n'eke — God the Creator.

Chukwu bi n'Elu — God who lives on high.

Danshiki — a smaller, more casual form of the *agbada*, usually worn within one's immediate neighborhood; (Hausa).

Dibia — a healer and diviner who uses an ability to commune with the gods both for medical purposes and for discerning the future.

Dim Onyeka -Lord of the Buzzing Bees — the chief god of the Nakanu clan whose reputation includes an arsenal of bees with which evil-doers are punished.

Ebie — a poetic tribute to a dearly beloved by a close relative.

Efulefu — a fool.

Eko — the old name for Lagos; (Yoruba).

Ekwe Mgba — the major hollowed-out, wooden musical instrument central to the special music of the wrestling match.

Eze — King or high chief.

Ibi N'Ukpabi — an oracle of justice who played a significant role during the slave trade: guilty supplicants were sent down the river to be sold; also known in European writings as the Long Juju at Arochukwu.

Igbo-ama-eze! — the Igbo recognize no overlords.

Ike, V.C. — contemporary Nigerian novelist, author of Toads for Supper, his best-known work; his later works use such terms as "whitemail" instead of "blackmail," as part of the revisionist use of language by people of color concerned about the imagery of black as evil, so current in the English language and in Western culture.

Ikem Issa — title meaning "Strength of the Issa People".

Isi Dim/ Eze Dim — the high priest of Dim Onyeka

Izaga — the stilt masquerade.

Jigida — beads worn by women around the waist.

Kobo — the lowest denomination in the Nigerian currency; equivalent to a penny. (Hausa origin).

Lappa — corruption of wrapper, the full-length woven cloth worn by African women from the waist down, across the neck, or in a variety of combinations.

Lolo — the goddess of the Nakanu.

Mazi — honorific form of "Mr."; equivalent to a self-conscious "Sire" (Igbo).

Mbamiri — the riverain communities of the lower Niger basin.

Mbara — open farmland, a form of the commons parceled out to lineages, who then subdivide them among family units; reverts back to lineage if not inherited.

Molue — a medium-sized bus with attributes similar to the bolekaja (Yoruba).

Naira — the basic Nigerian currency, comprised of 100 kobo.

Nakanu — the sub-clan on whom the tale is centered.

Nakanu Omere-Dike — Nakanu, surpriser of the over-confident.

Ndi Igbo — Igbo people.

Ngwu Eglege — a spear-like symbol of authority with tiny bells strewn all around it; carried by the Isi Dim.

Nza — a tiny but agile bird, prevalent in Igbo mythology.

Nze-n'Ozo — the leaders of a typical Igbo gerontocracy: the titled elders and the high-achieving younger men who attained *ozo* title ranks and became members of the sacred societies.

Nza n'Oba — legendary age when men amd animals were neighbors and shared similar experiences.

Nwoke-Ebube-Dike — great man full of the wonders of the strong.

Oba — king, ruler of a paramountcy among the Yoruba and the Bini, but also among the Onitsha Igbo.

Oga — a girls' sport involving simultaneous clapping, hopping, and keeping count; occasionally a song; often a mystery to boys.

Ogwugwu Dim — the abode of bee-god Dim Onyeka.

Ojare — expression of contempt; Yoruba, but popular in the South in sentence endings.

Oji Ofo — a select group of the oldest men in a typical Igbo lineage, deemed close to the ancestors, hence responsible for basic sacrifices that do not involve divination.

Okoso — a game of spinning tops, often fashioned from snail shells, or in later times, aluminium foil.

Oparamba Opara El'Igwe — names of deities, owners of streams and rivulets, among the Ehime clan; of far lower rank than the dreaded *Dim Onyeka*, these nevertheless are capable of creating illnesses and other discomforts, but also such joyful acts as incarnating as newborns.

Orie-Ndi-Agu — the market of a clan whose totem is the lion.

Osimiri — sea, large rivers like the Niger.

Ose — pepper spice.

Oyiri-di-ya — a wife who 'resembles' her husband.

Ozo-Di-Mgba — a nickname for the gorrilla, an animal in folklore that is known to wrestle with and triumph over the best wrestlers; literally, master wrestler.

Raffia — a form of palm whose sap, fermented and made into wine, is highly regarded.

Red Caps — chiefly caps depicting certain rank.

Ukwa — the breadfruit tree whose little seeds yield succulent beans that can be made into a porridge delicacy; a special family treat.

Ugbaka — a form of the oil-bean tree whose seeds, when matured in the dry season, split with an explosive sound, scattering their nutritious fruit for picking.

Umu Chukwu — Children of the High God — (see *Ibi N'ukpabi*); another name for the Aro.

Whaar! — the usual response of the audience; see *Chapkii*.

Zimbabwe stones — the ruins of ancient Zimbabwe.

African Studies
Educational Resource Center
-100 International Building
Michigan State University
East Lansing, MI 48824